Second Hand

Goods

Nurse Hal Among The Amish

Book 9

I0666424

Fay Risner

Fay Risner's books

Nurse Hal Among The Amish Series

A Promise Is A Promise   *Doubting Thomas*
The Rainbow's End   *Amish Country Arson*
Hal's Worldly Temptations   *Second Hand Goods*
As Her Name Is So Is Redbird
Emma's Gossamer Dreams
The Courting Buggy

Amazing Gracie Historical Mystery Series

Neighbor Watchers   *Poor Defenseless Addie*
Specious Nephew   *Will O Wisp*
The Country Seat Killer
The Chance Of A Sparrow
Moser Mansion Ghosts
Locked Rock, Iowa Hatchet Murders

Westerns

Stringbean Hooper Westerns   *Tread Lightly Sibby*
The Dark Wind Howls Over Mary   *The Blue Bonnet-novella*
Small Feet's Many Moon Journey   *A Coffin To Lie On-novella*
Ella Mayfield's Pawpaw Militia-Civil War

Christmas books

Christmas Traditions - An Amish Love Story   *Christmas With Hover Hill*
Leona's Christmas Bucket List

Fiction

Listen To Me Honey – novella   *Cowboy Girl Annie -novella*
Robot Grandma - novella

Children Books

Spooks In Claiborne Mansion   *My Children Are More Precious Than Gold*
Mr. Quacker

Nonfiction about Alzheimer's disease

Open A Window - Caregiver Handbook
Hello Alzheimer's Goodbye Dad-author's true story

Cookbook

Midwest Favorite Lamb Recipes

Renee Brown Mystery Series

The Answering Machine Knew   *One Big Bat*

Historical Fiction

The Cavorter   *The Coffin With A Window - Novella*

Books published by Booksbyfay Publisher

Romance
Sunset Til Sunrise On Buttercup Lane by Connie Risner

Military-nonfiction-Vietnam War
Redcatcher MP by Mickey Bright

Reader Reviews for Amish Country Arson

I absolutely loved that book and think it was one of the best yet! And I like the sentences you use. For example - Darkness was good for what was about to happen. And the one about how Hal calls herself a nurse and describes her as the woman with a man's name.

I liked how you got inside the mind of the arsonist and told her thoughts and made a person understand what was going on in her head.

Homey touch to have Biscuit pee on the back wheel of the buggy or whatever it was. I was glad to have Aunt Tootie still be visiting in the story and glad to have Tom Turkey still do some antics before his death. And I'm glad he died saving Hal rather than having the family decide they needed him for a meal.

Interesting mystery to wonder what dug the marigolds. I'm pleased you remembered to add the skunk to this story. And not just have it dig things and stink, but have Hal think she killed it. You made it an exciting adventure and not just a skunk incident.

I laughed at Hal's first impression of Wanda - that she would get along well with Stella for a neighbor. And I laughed at the thought of the bishop coming to see for himself if Gladys was able to come to church. It's a good thing preachers don't do that to their congregations - but maybe they should. Perhaps then folks would think twice about missing services.

The order at the sale when they sold everything before they got to the rooster Hal wanted - that reminds me of me. Seems things I'm interested in are always saved for a good while. That was funny how Tom Turkey treated the rooster. And it served Tootie right the way the rooster treated her.

That was so clever of you to have John ask the bishop to preach a sermon against modern conveniences in order to convict the young people. The barn raising, sorghum making, benefit sale - you really made those come to life. You didn't just pass over them in generalizations, but you described them down to the smallest details. Made me feel I was attending them.

I had forgotten about Eli Yutzy. So when I got to the mention of him, I thought perhaps he was the arsonist. And in my wildest dreams, I never guessed the arsonist would turn out to be a woman.

He healeth the brokenhearted and bindeth up their wounds. He determines the number of the stars and calls them each by name. Great is our Lord and mighty in power. His understanding has no limit. The LORD sustains the humble but casts the wicked to the ground.

Psalm 147:3 - 6

Chapter 1

Sharp honks, fairly low overhead, made brown haired Emma Keim peer up through the buggy windshield toward the cloud pocked sky. She saw a flock of geese flapping their way north over her buggy. A blob of white and dark green goo splattered on the windshield and slid downward leaving a two colored streak.

Emma frowned as she squinted her gray-green eyes up to follow the dark, feathered V shape. "Sure enough, that goose must be proud of himself for hitting his target from so high in the sky."

Otherwise, spring made for pleasant drives with plenty to see. Baby calves chased each other across pastures, causing cows to bellow worried bawls. Horses bucked and kicked their back feet high in the air as they raced after each other. Herds of freshly sheared sheep snipped at tender grass blades while the lambs nursed with tails wiggling.

Emma was on her way home from teaching school. Her father and stepmother's farm, John and Hallie Lapp, was just ahead of her. She really should stop and see how Hallie was feeling now that she was in her seventh month.

At the sight of a buggy slowing down on the road, Biscuit, the family's cream colored hound rose from beside the barn. He barked and stretched at the same time as he warned the house company was coming. After Emma pulled back on the reins and stopped, he ran to meet her buggy. Biscuit circled around it while he sniffed each wheel and lifted his leg to pee on a back one.

The muffled beat of her horse's hooves made enough noise without Biscuit's help to announce her arrival. The small faces of her little sisters. Redbird and Beth, peered out the window. She parked and stepped from her enclosed buggy as the front door swung open.

Curly, red headed Redbird's shrill, excited voice shouted, "Mama, Emma's here."

Brown haired Beth's softer voice called, "Hi, Emma."

The girls opened the screen door and rushed to the edge of the porch with their arms out for a hug. When Emma looked up, Hal stood with her arms folded over her chest in the doorway, smiling at her. "Girls, you don't have a coat on. It's too cool to stay out here. How about coming back into the house to talk to Emma?"

"Gute idea," Emma agreed as she ushered the three year olds inside. She gave Hallie a hug before she shrugged out of her black wool coat and hung it and her bonnet on the wall pegs. With a finger, she poked stray light brown wisps of hair back under her prayer cap.

"Come in the kitchen," Hal invited, smoothing the wrinkles out of her navy blue apron which made her protruding stomach noticeable. "I hoped you would stop by for a visit soon. How are you feeling?"

"Big." Emma chuckled. She rubbed her green dress, causing her expanding stomach to be noticeable and felt the baby kick.

"Tell me about it. Me, too," Hal commiserated as she led the way to the kitchen.

The girls followed and climbed up in chairs. They stayed on their knees and put their elbows on the table with their chins in their folded hands.

Emma pulled a chair away from the table to give her stomach room and eased herself down.

"Emma, you appear to be as far along as I am, and I should

deliver around mid June. We didn't think you should be. Maybe I should get out my doptone and check your baby," Hal suggested.

"Ach, I do not think you need to bother. For sure, I am two months behind your delivery date which makes it mid August. I only stopped by on my way home from school to see how you are feeling," Emma protested, noting the copper red curls escaping from Hal's prayer cap gave her a frazzled look. "Sure enough, you do not have as long to go as me. I am sure of that."

"Nah, but I know the baby is doing okay, because I use my doptone on myself routinely." Hal sheepishly admitted, "I grow tired so easily now. Sometimes, I take a nap when the girls nap. Afterwards, I feel guilty that I slept when I have work to do."

Emma shook her head and urged, "You should rest when you feel the need. The work will always be there and get done eventually."

"That's what I tell myself, but I've seen how many Amish women work recht up to the last minute before they give birth. Now I catch myself wondering how they do it. Would you like a cup of coffee?"

"Nah, I gave up coffee because of indigestion. I would take a cup of tea though if you do not make it too strong," Emma suggested.

"That would be gute. I could drink a cup of tea myself," Hal agreed.

She poured hot water from the teakettle into a stainless steel quart pan and added tea leaves. She left the tea to steep and turned to Emma. "Just to stop my curiosity about how my first grandbaby is doing, why don't we go into the clinic and check you out?"

Emma gave an exaggerated sigh. "I suppose you will not let me rest until we do."

Hal grinned. "Nah."

Once Emma was on the clinic bed with her stomach exposed, Redbird said, "It is fun to hear a baby's heartbeat."

Beth readily agreed. "Jah, Mama lets us listen to Redbird and my baby's heartbeat. It is really loud."

Emma's eyebrows went up at Hal. "Their baby?"

Hal put her hand up by her face and kept her voice low. "Technically, this is their father and my baby, but the girls said if they were going to help me with this baby he or she should be theirs. Why not?"

Emma smiled. "That's one way to get helpers."

"No flies on this mother," Hal joked as she scooted a chair over close to the bed.

She got her nurse's bag from the cupboard and pulled the doptone out. She laid the doptone on Emma's bare stomach, and right away they heard the swoosh-swoosh of placental blood flow, rushing in and out of the cord. Louder than the swooshes came the drumming sound of the fetal heartbeats. The doptone magnified the thumping beats, making them easily heard by Emma and her audience. The count of the beats registered on the box's screen.

Hal moved the doptone away from the middle, expecting to hear only softer swooshes. She picked up heartbeats, only not as strong this time. She was excited and worried at the same time, but she tried not to show it while she gave herself a silent lecture. What she heard was two different heartbeats, but one sounded weak.

So much for trying to keep her composure when examining a patient. She'd always been good at doing her job. This time should be no exception just because Emma was family. She rolled her lips together as she told herself she had to stay strong and professional.

"Was ist letz?" Emma asked sharply.

Hal took a deep breath and said calmly, "Nothing is wrong. The doptone just picked up two separate heartbeats."

Emma's hands flew to her cheeks as she gasped. "Ach! Are you sure?"

"Jah, the beats registered separately on the screen. Only one heart was fainter than the other," Hal said, concentrating on putting away the doptone.

"What does that mean?" Emma demanded.

"Ach, don't start worrying. One baby must be behind the other one. No wonder you're getting as large as me already.

Two babies would explain it," Hal declared.

Redbird suddenly caught on to what her mother meant. She shrieked, "You are having two babies, Emma!"

"Sure enough sounds like it," Emma agreed, still trying to digest Hal's information.

Redbird grabbed Beth's arm and pulled her into the living room.

"Now what's that all about?" Hal watched the girls disappear.

Emma glanced at Hal as she straightened her clothes into place. "Do not worry. You will find out soon enough."

"You're recht, but do I want to know?" Hal sat on the bed beside Emma. "So we have to change the birthing plan if I'm recht, young lady. No home delivery for you. Too many problems can happen during a twins delivery. I want you to go to Doctor Burns recht away. If I am recht, be prepared for the doctor to tell you to go to the hospital when those babies decide to come. Keep in mind your labor might begin early. It sometimes does with twins when they run out of room," Hal explained.

Emma frowned her dislike at the idea of going to Doctor Burns. She planned to help Hal when her time came in June. In return, Emma had her heart set on a home delivery with Hal's help. Nurse Hal gave her a narrowed eyed no nonsense look. "All recht, Hallie. I will talk to Adam tonight."

"Don't start fretting yet. Make an appointment with Doctor Burns. He will know what's best. Now, seems to me I remember I fixed tea. Let's have a cup. It is surely cool enough to drink by now," Hal said, thinking a change in subjects was a good idea.

Back in the kitchen, Emma sat, and the girls climbed into the chairs beside her.

Hal poured the tea in the cups. "How is it to teach in the new school?"

"I like the new Timberview School building very much. It is much handier than the old school. Sure beats going up and down the stairs to the loft in Adam's furniture shop when we used it for a makeshift school. Although, now I have to hook up the buggy and drive to school instead of taking the short walk through the timber." She giggled. "Listen to me complain. The scholars are proud of their school, and that is gute." Emma ducked her head when her eyes moistened.

"I'm sure they are. Why are you tearing up?" Hal asked with concern in her blue green eyes.

"I just reminded myself this is my last term to teach. Only two more weeks left. I already know I will miss teaching." Emma gave Hal a weak smile. "Remember how nervous I was before my first term. I never thought then I would ever say I would miss teaching when I had to stop."

"Oh, how well I remember. You were a basket case." Hal patted Emma's hand after she set a cup of steaming tea in front of her. "When you feel sad just think about those babies coming soon. You will be too busy to miss teaching."

"Jah, I know," Emma agreed, wrapping her hands around her cup. It seemed like it had been a very long day. She was ready for hot tea.

Hal turned to the little girls. "Redbird and Beth, would you like something to drink? You can have hot chocolate."

"Jah, Mama," Redbird chirped.

"Me, too," Beth said quietly.

As Hal made the girls each a drink from warm milk and instant chocolate powder, they stared at Emma. Hal set the two cups of hot chocolate on the table. The girls ignored the cups as they continued to stare at Emma.

Finally, Emma asked, "All recht, was ist los? Why are you girls looking a hole through me?

Redbird took a drink of her hot chocolate instead of answering right away. She turned, her deep blue eyes serious as she concentrated on Emma. Beth imitated her sister, taking a drink.

Emma found it hard to keep from smiling at the serious looks when she saw their chocolate mustaches. "Was ist letz?"

Redbird too a deep breath and answered in a rush of words, "Beth and I want to know if we can have one of your babies?"

"What?" Emma gasped, looking from one small head

bobbing up and down to the other.

Beth explained, "We decided if we had one of yours then we'd both have a baby, and I would not have to share Mama's baby with Redbird."

Hal set her tea cup down and shook her finger at the girls. "That will do!"

Emma laughed. "It is all recht, Hallie. Girls, that would be a gute idea, except I do not think Adam would like me to give away one of the babies. He will want me to share both of them with him. Sorry, but you girls will just have to share Mama's baby."

Redbird drank the last of her chocolate and chirruped like a robin, "Mama, you got something for us to do?"

"We want to help you while you talk to Emma," Beth said timidly.

Hal spoke slowly while she came up with an idea that the girls could handle, "Well, let's see. That's such a nice offer. How about I get each of you a dust rag? Want to dust the living room furniture for me?"

"Jah," Redbird cried.

Hal went to the mudroom and came out with two rags. "Here you go. Denki for helping me."

The girls accepted the rags and took off.

Emma hissed, "Do girls' voices ever change like boys do?"

"A little I suppose. Why?" Hal asked as she sat in her chair.

"I can hardly wait for Redbird's voice to go down an octave or two," Emma whispered.

"I know what you mean. I'll have to work on her to get her to lower her voice without hurting her feelings when the new baby is sleeping," Hal agreed as she listened to the girls chatter in the living room.

"Remember when we used to scold Daniel for slamming the door when he came in and out which woke up the girls," Emma brought up.

"Do I, and he still does it. I'm glad you reminded me. I'll have to work on him before June, sure enough," Hal declared. "Now, where was I? Oh jah, I have an applesauce cake in the oven. Don't let me forget to check on it in about fifteen minutes."

Emma did a keen assessment of Hal. "Hallie, are you sure you are feeling all recht?"

Hal looked over her tea cup at Emma. "Jah, I guess I'm just worried. It shows, huh?"

"Nothing is wrong with your pregnancy, ain't so?" Emma asked in alarm.

Chapter 2

"Nah, I'm doing just fine. Truthfully, I'm worried about your grandparents and Aunt Tootie." A grin flickered across Hal's face. "Now there's something to marvel at. Did you ever think you would hear me say I'm worried about Aunt Tootie?"

"I agree. Was ist letz with them?" Emma asked.

"I wish I knew. Maybe nothing," Hal wrapped her hands around her cup and took a sip. "Mom usually writes me once a month, and I write her back recht away so she doesn't worry about me and this baby I'm carrying. This time it's been two months and no letter from her. I wonder if one of them might be sick with the flu or worse."

"You can always go to the phone shed and call Mammi," Emma suggested. "Better yet, you can use your cell phone. No one but me and you would know."

"Jah, the cell phone is the most convenient for me recht now. I'll do that soon if I don't hear from Mom. The mailman stopped this afternoon, but I haven't been to the mailbox yet to see if I got a letter," Hal said.

Emma stood up slowly. "You check on that cake in the oven and finish your tea while I go see what the mailman left. I will pray as I walk to the mailbox that you have a letter, and it will be gute news."

Redbird and Beth stopped in the kitchen door.

"You leaving, Emma?" Redbird asked.

"Nah, not yet. I am going to the mailbox for your mama,"

Emma told her.

Redbird said, "That is gute. Mama, we are done. Can we go upstairs and dust?"

"Sure you can, but go out on the front porch first and shake those rags to get rid of the dust on them," Hal instructed. "My, it is so nice to have such gute helpers. When you get that dusting job done, you can play."

Emma stopped long enough to put on her bonnet and coat. The girls followed her out on the porch. "Sisters, you are gute helpers. Your mama needs all the help you can give her recht now. Soon she will give you a baby to help her take care of."

"I want a sister," Redbird chirped.

"A brother would be nice," Beth said. "Noah and Daniel are too big to play with us."

"We do not get to choose, but I promise you, boy or girl, you will like either one," Emma declared. "Now I have to go get the mail for Mama. You shake your rags gute and hard."

A gust of north wind pushed Emma down the driveway and swirled last year's leaves in front of her sensible black shoes. The stiff breeze sure didn't feel like spring had arrived. April in Iowa made a habit of changing from chilly to warm and back. Even the pair of robins under the clothesline puffed up like they were cold.

Joseph, Hal's araucana rooster, huddle in the middle of his flock over by the barn. The chickens were too cold to scratch for bugs. She gathered her coat around her and hurried. When she opened the lid, a white envelope shined at her in the dimly lit mailbox. Emma saw the return address was Mammi's. At first, she was excited. As she shut the mailbox lid, she remembered to pray that the letter didn't hold bad news. *Lord, Hallie needs nothing to upset her recht now. Please make this letter gute news. Amen.*

The sound of a car behind her made Emma glanced over her shoulder, so she'd know she was off to the side of the road far enough. She was so she started back to the house. The bright red sports car's tires made soft crunching sounds in the gravel, creeping nearer to her.

The car, with the top down, pulled close to Emma. She

frowned, not liking the fact the car didn't stay out in the road where it belonged.

"Good afternoon." The man smiled, showing straight white teeth. "I wondered if there was garden produce in your stand for sale yet."

Taken aback, Emma studied the young man. He wore a crisp, white shirt and dark trousers and no coat. Clearly not the hands of a working man on the shiny black steering wheel, but one with money to afford a manicure to go along with his fancy car. He stopped so close she got a whiff of a mixture of cigarette smoke and strong scented cologne.

This time of year the stand doors were closed. Emma thought all he had to do was look to see that. This Englisher was not a gardener, or he'd know this wasn't produce time. "Nah, this is not the selling season. We have very little in gardens around here yet, and most of those plants are under gallon milk jugs until the danger of frost is gone."

"Ah, well, there you have me. We just made it through winter, didn't we?" The man, about her age, said as he studied her closely.

Actually the look made her think he was inspecting her. That was enough to make Emma walk away. She didn't like to be rude to anyone, but she wanted to end the conversation with this stranger. The man put his car in gear. Emma walked faster, but he drove slowly beside her again. The cold tone in his voice gave Emma a creepy feeling of beware. "I'm just out for a ride. Like my car?"

Emma shook her head once for yes without looking at him and kept walking.

"Would you like to go for a ride in this car? That should be a treat for you, right?" The man asked. To Emma he sounded condescending like riding in his car would be doing her a favor.

"I am busy. Excuse me," Emma said curtly as she turned into the driveway.

The man looked familiar, but she couldn't remember where she'd seen him. She hoped the Englisher would drive away if she stopped talking to him. The car stopped. Emma kept walking, hoping she made it to the porch and inside if he intended to keep coming after her.

"Hey, those cute little girls on the porch yours?" The driver called.

Redbird and Beth continued to shake their dust rags as they waited for Emma. Uneasy that he asked about her small sisters, she ignored him. "Girls, you have the dust rags clean enough now. Go on inside out of this wind. It is too cold to stay out here without your coats on." She had a hard time keeping urgency out of her voice.

Redbird frowned as she glanced at the red car and back. "Who was that man talking to you?"

"I do not know. He did not tell me his name. Quick about it now," Emma replied, pushing the girls ahead of her.

After she shut the door, she peeked over the half curtain on the living room window. The red car picked up speed and roared on toward the highway, leaving a cloud of dust in his wake for as far as she could see.

Emma took her coat and bonnet off and hung them on a peg as the girls tromped up the stairs. When she entered the kitchen, Hal laughed. "Oh how I wish I had as much energy again as those two live wires."

"Me, too." Emma waved the letter at Hal. "You have that letter you were waiting for."

Hal pushed a saucer and fork over by a steaming cup. "Tea is in the cups again. I thought you might need a refill to warm you up from the walk to the mailbox, and I cut a piece of warm cake for each of us. What took you so long to get to the mailbox and back?"

"An Englisher stopped to ask if the vegetable stand was open yet?"

"That's very peculiar. It's too early for a vegetable stand to open," Hal said.

"I told him so," Emma replied.

"Sit down while I see what's going on in Titonka. The letter should be a large one after two months. Mom likes to tell me news about what everyone in town has done lately." Hal tore open the envelope. She pulled the paper out and unfolded it. "Ach, it's just one page."

Emma thought a quick prayer again for no bad news as she sipped her tea and watched Hal scan the page.

"Oh, my," Hal said on a gust of air.

Emma didn't think Hallie looked too upset, but she wished her step-mother would read faster and tell her what was so interesting in the letter. Her curiosity was about to get the better of her.

"Now isn't that something?" Hal declared to herself as she continued to read.

"Hallie, I will die of curiosity if you do not stop this. What is in that letter that is so interesting, please and denki," Emma declared.

"All recht, I've got the letter scanned. I read so fast I must go back and reread it again. Your grandparents are selling their farm and moving. So is Aunt Tootie," declared Hal.

"Nah! That explains why they have been busy. I suppose at their age it is time they moved to town," Emma surmised.

"Ach, Titonka isn't where they're moving," Hal said, smiling from ear to ear. "They're moving here to live. They want us to find them an acreage so they can have a garden and a small pasture. An acreage with a grossdawdi house, because Aunt Tootie is coming with them."

"Will wonders never cease," Emma said in amazement. "I prayed for gute news, but never in my wildest dreams did I expect this. Why would they move here and leave their friends?"

"Mom says they miss all of us when they aren't here and want to live near their grandchildren. She'd be able to help me when the baby comes, and you too if you want help.

They have made many friends here and enjoy themselves every time they visit in the summer. Wickenburg has become a second home so they might as well move here.

Mom says Aunt Tootie said she wouldn't stay in Titonka without them. She has made friends here and wouldn't mind living near us. We are the only family she has. Looks like we need to start house hunting times two."

Emma asked, "How much time do we have to look for a place?"

"They will arrive the end of April. Dad is renting a moving van and will drive it himself. Mom will follow in the car with Aunt Tootie."

"Ach, that is too soon. I do not know if we will find them a place in time," Emma gasped.

"They know they can stay with us until one is available," Hal said. "Oh, Emma, I'm so happy recht now."

Emma laughed. "I can see that. I am glad the letter held gute news. Praise the Lord, my prayer by the mailbox was answered even better than I would have ever dreamed. Now I must head for home. I do not like to drive on the road in the dark by myself anymore. Sure enough, Adam will be home soon and want his supper."

As Hal followed Emma into the living room, she tapped her lips with a finger. "Speaking of Adam, he's a gute one to ask about places for sale. He's always busy with his carpenter jobs and hears news from everyone, ain't so"

"Jah, that is a gute idea. I will be sure to ask him and let you know," Emma said as she put on her coat and bonnet.

"Here," Hal said, handing Emma a plate wrapped in a towel. "Two pieces of cake for dessert tonight. One less thing you will have to worry about cooking after a long day."

*   *   *

Emma couldn't wait to tell Adam all her news. She pulled in front of Keim's Furniture Shop and got out. The clerk Priscilla Tefertiller's fiberglass buggy was still at the shop. Her horse grazed in the grassy pen. He nickered at her horse, raced to stick his head over the split rail fence and lifted his tail to drop a pile.

It was after five, and Priscilla usually left for home by now. Since she was still at the shop, maybe she'd have an idea how long before Adam would quit for the night.

When Emma burst through the door, she was in for a surprise. Adam's brother, slender, tall, dark haired, Bobby Keim leaned on the counter, holding hands with Priscilla on the other side. The bell above the door jingled. Bobby turned loose of Priscilla's hands like he'd been jolted by an electric fence, straightened up and turned around to face Emma.

No wonder Priscilla is still here. Bobby has her occupied. Emma greeted, "Gute afternoon, you two. Priscilla, I wondered if you have any idea when Adam will be home."

Willowy shaped Priscilla tried to hide her red face with her hands. "When he left here this morning, his job was for the Weber sisters. They wanted a built in cupboard in the old kitchen. I'd say as fast as Adam is he should be done and on his way home unless the Weber sisters delayed him. You know how particular they are."

Bobby chuckled as he pushed his straw hat up and let a shock of dark hair fall on his forehead. "Jah, but they may treat Adam to one of their delicious desserts. He's not one to refuse their food, ain't so?"

"Sure enough, and he should not," Emma said. "The Weber sisters are gute customers. Adam and you built them a whole second kitchen already. He would hate to hurt their feelings by turning down their cooking."

"That is sure enough," Bobby agreed as his dark eyes grew intense. Bobby's serious natured expression was the one Emma was used to seeing. She couldn't remember the last time Bobby laughed or looked happy until just now. He studied Emma and held his head over one shoulder. "You look flushed. Was ist letz?"

"Nah, nothing is wrong. Something is very recht. I am bursting to tell someone. You two will have to do for recht now until Adam shows up. Hallie had a letter from her folks. They are selling their farm in northern Iowa and moving down here to live by us. Aendi Tootie is coming with them. We are so pleased they will be living close by," Emma gushed.

"That is a very voonderball gute thing with babies coming in the family. Those two women will be gute helpers," Priscilla agreed.

"They want a large acreage. One with a grossdawdi house for Aendi Tootie to live in. So if you hear of one let us or Hallie know," Emma said.

Bobby gave her a humble smile. "Sure enough, I will."

"Now I am going home and fix supper," Emma declared. She opened the door to go out, turned around and smiled at the couple. "I am so sorry I interrupted your very important conversation." As the red faced couple could do more than stumble over an answer, she rushed to her buggy.

Emma hurried to unhitch her horse, take off the harness and grain him. She was in the house in a few minutes, had the wood cookstove fire burning, washed her hands and put on an apron. In no time, she hummed as she turned potatoes frying in a cast iron skillet.

She smiled as she thought about how Adam looked at her like she was crazy when she asked him to take the gas cookstove out of their new home and put in a wood cookstove. It didn't take her long to discover she'd cooked on the wood stove so long she couldn't get used to the gas stove. Besides, somehow it seemed too English to have such a modern stove.

The living room door opened and closed. Emma tossed the turner on a plate and rushed to the kitchen doorway.

Dark wavy haired Adam, a head taller than Emma, gave her a wave and a good natured smile that settled in his dark eyes. For some women it might be daunting to have a husband that couldn't talk. Not so for Emma. She felt so close to her husband they knew what each other was thinking without talking. What Adam needed to convey he wrote on a pad he carried in his shirt pocket.

She ran to the gentle man who stood a head taller than her. She loved him so much and hugged him to show it, feeling the strength of his broad shoulders as he hugged her back. "I'm so glad you are home."

He pulled her away, and his eyebrows shot up in question.

"I am fine. Do not fret so. Wait until you hear all my news. Do not frown like that. The news is gute," Emma reassured him.

Adam put his hands together as if he was washing them.

"Ach, go wash your hands while I see to my skillets, but hurry up," Emma ordered. "Supper is almost ready. I stopped to see how Hallie is doing. She gave me fresh applesauce cake, so I did not have to fix a dessert. I can tell you some of my news while you wash, but I have so much to tell it will take a while."

Adam wet his hands and soaped them, listening to Emma chatter. He dried his hands as she said, "Sure enough, if you hear of such an acreage let Daed and Hallie know."

Adam grinned as he took his notepad and pencil out of his pocket. "I already know a place."

Emma gasped as she read. "Where?"

Adam wrote, "Just past the Mast place. Jake Fisher wants to move to his son's farm ten miles from where he lives. Remember his wife, Metta, passed away six months ago. He is getting older and does not want to live alone anymore. The home place has a grossdawdi house."

"Voonderball gute, just what Dawdi needs," Emma exclaimed. "I best finish setting the table. Supper is ready."

Adam scribbled again on his notepad and grabbed her arm. "When I drive by the farm, the houses look run down. Your dawdi might think it will take more work and expense to fix them up then they are worth."

"Ach," Emma said, disappointed. "All recht, just keep your eyes open for other places. Dawdi can decide what works for him when he gets here."

While they ate, Emma kept looking at Adam as she chewed.

Finally, Adam took his notepad out and wrote, "You look like you are about to pop with more news. Was ist letz?"

Emma gushed, "Just before I came home, I stopped by the shop to see if you were back. It was after five, and Priscilla was still there,"

Adam wobbled his hand and kept eating.

"Ach! I didn't think there was anything wrong with that. It was a voonderball gute thing." Emma gave Adam a wide smile.

Adam wobbled his hand again with one eyebrow up.

"Bobby was there. He was visiting with Priscilla. Your brother seemed the happiest I have seen him in ages. Did you know he has taken a liking to Priscilla?"

Adam shrugged.

"Sure enough, you should pay more attention to what is going on with your brother," Emma complained. "They seemed very close. That is a gute thing. Priscilla has grown up and needs to settle down. So does Bobby. I did not think I would ever see him smile again or find another woman to love after Annie died," Emma said and added, "But he has."

Adam nodded he agreed as he laid his fork on his empty plate.

"Now before we have the cake Hal gave us, there is one more bit of news I received at Hallie's this afternoon." Emma paused as she studied Adam.

He took his notepad out of his shirt pocket again and wrote, "You really are full of news. Tell me." He picked up his coffee cup and took a sip.

"Hallie thought I looked like I was as advanced in my pregnancy as she is which I know is not so. Nothing would do but she had to check the baby's heartbeat with her doptone. Adam, she heard … I mean we heard two different heartbeats. Hallie says we are having twins."

Adam choked as he swallowed and sputtered a spray of coffee over the table. His face turned red as he tried to breathe while he had a coughing fit.

Emma got up and slapped him on the back, trying not to smile at his reaction. "I knew you would be as surprised by the news as I am." When Adam quieted down, she continued, "Hallie says I should go see Doctor Burns for a gute checkup and get his opinion. If it is really so that I am having twins, Hallie says I should go to the hospital to have them since having two babies at the same time could cause complications. Hallie does not want to help me with a home delivery."

With a shaky hand, Adam wrote, "Make an appointment for as soon as possible, and I will take you. Hal is recht. We need to be sure so we know how to plan."

"You all recht with having twins?" Emma asked as she sat back down.

Adam nodded and gave her a quivering smile from ear to ear.

"That is gute. If not, Redbird and Beth asked if they could have one of our babies since we are having two," Emma said.

Adam, with a twinkle in his eyes, wobbled his hand.

"I told them I would ask you, but I said I thought you would want me to share these babies with you. They will have to be satisfied with the one their mama has."

Adam winked at her.

Emma's eyes sparkled. "Gute, I hoped you would agree. So I am giving you fair warning, Redbird and Beth might not believe me. They might ask you for the final say. Those two can be very convincing. We need to stick together on what to say so they do not talk us out of one of our babies." She giggled as she returned his wink.

Chapter 3

After the worship service on Sunday, Bishop Elton Bontrager made the announcement teacher Emma Keim and her scholars were having an open house the last day of school on Friday next. The scholars would give tours of the new school. Everyone in the church community was invited to share the day so they might see the school. A potluck lunch for all and games for adults and scholars to make it a fun day. They should talk to teacher Emma Keim about details.

He added, "Teacher Emma wants it known that this will be her last term teaching. The directors will have to find a different teacher before school starts in the fall. If there is anyone among us who wants to talk to the directors about the job please do that soon."

The last day of school dawned sunny and warmer than usual for April. A perfect day for the new school's open house. Adam and Emma arrived early. Adam lit a fire in the stove to take the chill off the building and set up folding tables along the wall to place the food and drinks on.

The day before, Emma practiced with the students so they knew where to stand and what to say to the visitors. This last day of school was different from all the other potluck picnics. Many curious folks, Englishers and Amish would show up to see the new school. A building very much needed after the arsonist burned the school that had been used for years.

Timberview School
Emma Keim's New Amish School

The white entry door was different. This one had a glass in the top half on which Emma wrote greetings. *Let your smile change the world, but don't let the world change your smile.* Below that saying was another one. *In this classroom, you are important. You are loved. You are part of a team.*

Emma stationed herself outside to welcome people to Timberview School. She explained for the tour they were to stop to listen to the scholars as the children explained the fine points of the new school.

The children arrived early and took up their posts. John Mast, son of Ben and Edna, was the first scholar to greet people at the door. Emma picked him, because as an eighth grader, she felt he'd be comfortable welcoming everyone, and he had the longest speech.

When the first three couples came, John pointed as he spoke, "New in this school is the wooden wall that blocks the winter winds from coming in on the students when the door is opened. That makes the inside warmer for the scholars.

In the space between the wall and the outside door, you see a table for the water bucket, wash pan and soap. A peg above the table holds the towel to dry our hands. On the opposite side, metal clamps on the wall hold the mop, broom and dust pan that the scholars use to clean the school each day."

Another eighth grader, Malinda, daughter of Adin and Anna Bender explained the wall. "This wall serves a purpose besides blocking the wind. It has a shelf near the top to hold lunch coolers. Under the shelf are pegs for coats and hats. On the floor under the pegs are black plastic trays to place the winter boots in. That keeps the melting snow from running into puddles on the floor that we would step in and get wet socks.

The wall can be walked around on both ends as you can see. So you can go passed me and circle through the school to the other tour guides. You will come out the other end of the wall."

Sixth grader Jake, son of one of the school board directors, Amos Coblentz, was stationed at one end to show the line of people which way to enter. "Once you have the tour, the women can sit and visit while the men can go outside through the other end of the wall. Later, after you have had the tour and the scholars singing program is over, there will be a lunch served. In the afternoon will be softball and volleyball for those interested in forming teams to play against the scholars."

Sixth grader David Mullet, son of Hank and Mary, stood near the shelves filled with new books. "Adam Keim helped with the interior work so he built these library shelves under the windows. We are bless to have many new books to place on the shelf." David pointed to the back side of the wall. "No need at the back of the room for the wooden table where the scholars used to work together. Several folding tables have been donated. One of them can be unfolded and refolded later which is handy. Those tables are the same one that are used today for the food and drinks.

Two new shiny wooden benches built by Adam Keim are to sit on while we are at the tables. Visitors may use them while they visit during class to observe the scholars at work. The benches can be taken outside at lunch time today. For those people and others that brought folding chairs, they will be able to eat at tables the men set up which were made from boards laid on sawhorses. The two benches in here can be taken out as well to sit on in the shade."

Fifth grader Rose Yoder, the youngest child of Luke and Linda, said, "The rest is much the same as the old school only everything smells new. We breathe in deep every day to smell the new wood, and praise the Lord for having given such a nice school. We have neat rows of scholar desks, a teacher's desk up front on the riser with a bell on it so teacher can get our attention. There is the blackboard across the back wall with an alphabet border across the top. Above that in a row is the animal each scholar picked as his or her favorite to color and write their names on and the names of their parents. That everyone knows who the scholars were that went to school here this year."

On the blackboard, Emma had written the five values she taught to learn, practice and live by. Rose Yoder suggested the parents take a moment to read the list.

Number one was in Matthew. All things whatsoever ye

would have others do to you , do ye even so to them.

Number two: Cooperation – With each other when working together or at recess.

Number three: Respect – Learn to respect your parents, your teacher, other scholars, school property, other people's property and others' space and privacy.

Number four: Responsibility – All students must learn to help keep their school clean. Each child is given a work schedule for the week. One day is sweep the room, second is help the teacher check the work books, third is clean the blackboard and clap the erasers, fourth is empty trash cans and the scholar's fifth day is a day off. This schedule is alternated between the students.

Number five: Obedience – Scholars quickly learn the teacher means what she says. Otherwise, the children would soon be doing what they want.

When the room was wall to wall people, Teacher Emma announced it was time for the students to stand on the riser to sing three songs.

After the singing program was over, Emma excused them. She pointed to the blackboard where she'd written the five values that were practiced every day by her and the scholars. "When our children learn values at a young age, it helps them through life as a church member, an employee or employer, a teacher, a parent or in the ministry. It helps the teacher when the parents continue to practice these values at home.

The reason I bring this up now is that as most of you know this is my last term of teaching. I am thinking ahead to the next teacher and will leave these values on the blackboard for her to start her term with. Now it is lunch time, and the scholars are anxious to get on to the games this afternoon. Bishop Elton Bontrager will say a prayer to bless our new school and then the men can line up to eat first and the rest will follow."

As soon as the bishop's prayer ended, the line of men began. Across the room, Emma noticed the man, the driver of the red sports car, leaned against the wall. He was mingling with other Englishers friendly with the Amish. They were talking to Bishop Bontrager, her father, and Bobby Keim, but the young Englisher didn't seem to be listening to the conversation. He stared at her as if he enjoyed her watching him.

Emma made the mistake of observing him too long. The young man smiled at her and nodded, enjoying her attention. His cocky smile didn't make Emma one bit comfortable. She vowed to stay away from him. Even as she thought it, she knew that was a vow she couldn't keep. She had to serve cake at the dessert table.

The stranger finally had a chance to talk to her when he went through the food line. "Hello, so we meet again. It's nice to see you. I didn't know you're the teacher," he greeted in a low voice as if he was talking to a friend.

Emma glanced at his plate. Very small portions of baked beans, potato salad, peas and sloppy joe on a bun made her wonder why the man really showed up. He sure didn't come to eat, and he hadn't shown one bit of interest in the new school's tour.

"Which piece of cake would you like? Chocolate, white or applesauce cake?" She pointed at three rows of paper saucers with forks beside the cake.

"All the choices look so good. I think I'd like to try the applesauce cake. I've never had that before. Is that the one you would pick?" he asked, trying to keep up the conversation with her.

Emma said bluntly, "I am surprised to see you at this Amish school."

"I heard about an open house for the school. That was terrible news when someone burned the other building. I wanted to see the new school for myself and add to the school fund like many of the other people from town," he defended, A evil light glimmered in his eyes as he looked at her intensified Emma's uneasiness.

Emma held out a saucer of applesauce cake. He put his hand over her hand and clamped her fingers tightly to the saucer.

Emma hissed, "Let me go."

The man went on talking as if he hadn't heard her.

"Besides, I went to that fund raising event. I saw first hand how much fun you Amish can make an event, I couldn't pass this one up, either. It's an added bonus that I get to see and talk to you today."

Emma jerked her hand away. The saucer landed upside down on the table. She busied herself cleaning up the scattered cake pieces, refusing to look at him. He could get his own cake or move on.

As her face reddened with anger, she dumped the sticky crumbs and saucer into the waste can hidden under the table cloth. She looked up and he was still in front of her.

The man said snidely, "Sorry, my bad. I caused you to clean up a mess. I guess I didn't have too good a hold on that cake, did I? I'll choose another piece of applesauce cake."

He didn't sound the least bit sorry to Emma. She narrowed her eyes at him with her hands clutched together in front of her apron. She didn't want to give him the satisfaction of seeing her hands tremble "All recht, do so and leave. Others want to get through the food line." Her voice was icy sharp. Adam was next in line, watching Emma. He was very interested in what happened between her and the stranger.

Breathing easier as the man walked away, she tried to keep the nervousness out of her voice. "Adam, pick which cake you want, white, chocolate and applesauce."

Adam picked up a saucer with white cake on it, nodded toward the Englisher's back and wobbled his free hand.

"It's all recht. We can talk later." As she handed out cake to the rest of the line, she thought back to the fund raiser at the Yoder farm. That was where she'd seen the Englisher before. He appeared out of the crowd and watched her give Redbird and Beth a pony ride. When she noticed him leaning against a fence post, he struck up a conversation with her.

It made her uneasy now when she realized he showed up too frequently lately. She looked around the crowded room as she handed Abel Schrock a piece of cake, hoping the Englisher had left. No such luck. The man, leaning against the back wall, was still slowly eating his cake with his eyes on her.

She directed her attention back to serving. She didn't want

him to think she cared one way or the other that he was still in the room. He seemed to be a clean cut Englisher, but he had a disconcerting way of staring at her. Not to mention the fumes of cigarette smoke and strong cologne on his clothes that made her want to sneeze. She didn't like being in the same room with him.

The rest of the afternoon, children took turns telling Teacher Emma they were going to miss her. Marianne Coblentz gave her a hug. The curly haired blond was such a sweet child, and now in the third grade. As the girl told Emma how much she'd miss her, Emma reminded herself she might have been Marianne's stepmother if she'd consented to marrying Amos Coblentz.

Chapter 4

On the last Saturday in April an hour before lunch, Jim Lindstrom parked a large moving van in front of John Lapp's house behind Adam and Emma's buggy. Right behind him, Nora stopped their car.

Tootie, a shorter version of her sister only with her silver hair cut short and permed curly, came around the car. She joined Nora, her younger sister by two years. Hal's mother was solidly built and a head taller than Tootie. She kept her hair cut short which she felt was easier to care for. They walked over to the moving van and waited for Jim, Hal's father, to climb out.

A retired dairy and crop farmer, Jim loved country life. He stretched his broad shoulders and took in a deep breath. "Smell that fresh country air. I love it."

Tootie sucked in a breath. "Smells like cows and horses to me. Never considered that pleasant."

"Tootie, you breathed too deeply. I was smelling the fresh mowed lawn and food cooking," Jim cracked.

Nora scolded, "Jim."

"Don't bother, Nora. If he hasn't changed by now, he never will," observed Tootie cryptically.

"Anyway, I sure am glad to get out of that van and here all in one piece. I was getting stiff from all that sitting." Jim rubbed his bottom to prove it.

As they walked to the house, Biscuit yipped a greeting as he ran to them. The dog, with is long pink tongue lolling out of the side of his mouth, circled the three of them once and romped along by them. He looked happy to see them as if it had been just yesterday they went on a ride and were just getting home.

By that time, the whole Lapp family gathered on the porch to greet and hug the Lindstroms.

After the family had time to visit and eat lunch, Jim insisted he was eager to see Jake Fisher's farm right away.

John said he'd be glad to drive. As he rubbed his stomach, he added, "When I eat too much dinner, I get schlafferich (sleepy) soon so I should move around recht away once."

Hal declared it was a nice day for a drive in the country no matter where they went.

So the Lapp family, Jim, Nora and Aunt Tootie climbed into the buggy. Adam and Emma followed behind in their buggy so they could go on home afterward.

John Lapp, Hal's dark haired, dark eyed husband, turned to his father-in-law, on the seat beside him. "I should warn you Adam says the Fisher place might need too much fixing up to be worth what Jake is asking for it. You can stay with us as long as you need. That way we can keep our eyes open for other places for sale if you do not like this one."

"Sounds good," Jim agreed as he looked out the window at a black Angus cow calf herd grazing the crisp, spring grass of a hillside pasture. "I think this is about the prettiest country I've ever seen. So peaceful."

John smiled at him. "I do not know other places, but I agree with you about this one."

Jake Fisher came out on his porch to greet the visitors when the Lapp and Keim buggies drove in. The lanky fellow's bushy gray beard brushed the second button hole of his blue cotton shirt as he waved at the group coming toward him. He expected the company to be for a afternoon visit on this in between worship weekend.

As he went to meet them, he greeted, "Come visit a spell."

John took the lead. He shook hands with Jake and introduced him to the others. He explained to Jake that his in-laws had moved here and was looking for a place to buy that had a grossdawdi house on it. They heard his place was for sale.

In a husky, quiet voice, Jake said, "Jah, sure enough, I am selling just what you need. I will stay out of the way while you look around all you want." He followed the group up on the porch and sat down in his rocker.

The women stopped to look at the view before they went into the house. Noah and Daniel headed toward the outbuildings to check on the condition of the barn and chicken house.

Nora surmised, "My goodness, those two boys have grown up so fast. Noah is so tall now, and I love his deep voice. Daniel looks more like his father every day and going to catch up to Noah very soon."

Hal smiled. "We're very proud of our sons."

"You should be. They are two very nice young men," Tootie added as went inside with Jim, John and Adam following them.

Adam had been right about the buildings being run down. Though the place had pluses according to the Lindstroms. Jim and Nora liked that the house and land lay only four miles from Hal's home. They walked through the house and found it roomy with plenty of window light.

After looking around, the group went outside to compare notes on what they saw. Nora complained the three bedrooms upstairs and one down needed closet space for storage. The large kitchen needed more cupboard space.

Listening from his rocker, Jake offered to leave the cookstove. Nora said she'd be glad to use his cookstove. She thought it would be fun to cook with a wood stove again, and she'd had practice cooking on Hal's stove. Besides, as large as the kitchen was if she changed her mind, she could always set a modern stove beside the wood cookstove.

Jim noted the roof was in bad need of shingling or tin. A new roof and a coat of white paint would improve the looks of the outside of the house. He suggested maybe he could hire Noah and Daniel to climb the ladders to paint. He'd hire a roofer for the house roof. To which John replied Noah and

Daniel were good at roofing and could do that work for him, too.

The group walked over to the grossdawdi house. Tootie liked the front porch that ran the length of the house. It was ground level so she wouldn't have to worry about climbing steps. She thought about the fact the small house didn't have a basement under it. Now that did bother Tootie. "Where will I go during a storm? Remember the tornado that came through here? We took cover in John and Hallie's basement."

Nora answered softly, "That won't be a problem if Jim wants this place. You could come get in our basement with us any time you know there's a storm and sleep over at our house."

Once they were inside, they found one large room for the kitchen and living room and a long bedroom on the end of the living room. Aunt Tootie grumbled, "I will need an indoor bathroom."

"Yes, so will we," Nora told Jim.

Jim studied the bedroom. "This room is long enough to put a small bathroom on one end and still have room for the bed and a closet with drawers. What do you think, Tootie?"

"That works for me," Tootie agreed.

They walked back outside where John, Hal, Emma, Adam and Jake Fisher waited for them. "Well, what do you think, gals?" Jim asked Nora and Tootie.

"Is there enough ground to suit you?" Nora asked.

Jim turned to Jake, "How much land do you mean to see goes with the houses?"

Jake rubbed his beard as he thought. "How much you need?"

Jim looked at the grassy field that extended behind the barn. "How much is fenced in behind the barn to the creek?"

"Twenty acres," Jake said.

"You willing to sell that much?" Jim asked.

"Jah, if that will sell the place so I can move in with my son. He does not need the pasture, but he is going to farm the fields," Jake said honestly.

"That's quite a bit of money to tie up in fixing the houses

and outbuildings," Jim said, thinking out loud. "If we can make a deal on that much land, I still have to put out plenty for overhauling all the buildings if we can find a carpenter to do the job soon."

"Jah, I understand that," Jake agreed.

Jim winked at John. "You know any good carpenter close by to do the remodeling for us?"

"I'm sure there might be someone that would like your business," John said with a twinkle in his eyes. He turned to Adam. "You know a carpenter Jim can hire to work recht away?"

Adam looked at Jim and pecked himself in the chest with a finger.

Jim chuckled. "Good, Adam. The job is yours if you can start soon. We'd like to get moved in before winter. We can sit the furniture we brought in the middle of the rooms and leave it there until the work is done. It's costing me an arm and a leg every day while I have the rental truck."

Noah and Daniel joined them after looking at the barn and chicken house.

"There is twenty acres goes with the houses. Think this place will do, boys?" Jim asked.

"You need to get some work done on the barn and chicken house," Daniel said.

"Jah, both buildings could use mending. The barn would hold your horse and cow recht away, but coons and possums can get in the chicken house if you do not patch it first," Noah said.

Nora perked up. "What is this about a horse and cow?"

"If we're going to live here we need a horse to pull our buggy and plow up a garden spot. I figured the cow would be good for fresh milk. Chickens will give us fresh eggs, and all of it will be something to keep me busy," Jim explained.

"You have a horse at John's farm and a buggy," Nora said pointedly.

"I gave both of those to the boys. Remember? We need a larger buggy than the courting buggy to drive to town when we shop. That buggy is more suitable for these two young sprouts," Jim explained, winking at the boys.

Tootie piped up, "Isn't that what you have a car for?"

"The car will do on rainy days or in the winter. I just want to be like everyone else around here so we fit in. You know how it is. When in Rome do what the Romans do," Jim explained. "Speaking of fitting in, do we want electricity put in or have gas lamps and heat with gas and a generator for electricity."

"Whatever you think, Jim. We can always change our minds later," Nora said.

John suggested to Jim, "Are you sure you want to speak for this place before you have had a chance to look around the neighborhood?"

Nora, Tootie and Hal looked at Jim.

"I sure do like this place if the women are happy," Jim said as he studied his wife and sister-in-law. Nora and Tootie both agreed they liked the looks of the area.

The sale of the Fisher property to the Lindstroms was over with by the next week. John and his sons helped Jim carry the furniture into the houses so he could turn the moving van in at Wickenburg's U Haul Rental service. Nora drove behind Jim to pick him up.

The plan was for the Lindstroms and Tootie to stay with the Lapps until Adam had the work done on the big house. After the Lindstroms moved into their house, Tootie could stay with her sister and brother-in-law until the grossdawdi house was remodeled.

*   *   *

The next weekend was Gemeesunndaag, worship Sunday, at Levi and Linda Yoder's farm. Everyone at church were happy to see the Lindstroms and Tootie had returned.

Heavy set, short legged, red faced Bishop Bontrager greeted Jim Lindstrom with a smile as he shook hands. "How long you plan to stay this time?"

Jim replied, "We're here to stay. We bought Jake Fisher's place and some of his land. Tootie will be living in the grossdawdi house by us."

"I see. We wilcom you to the community," the bishop said as he shook hands with Jim.

Tootie was eager to visit with her friend Edna Mast so she looked along the women benches for her. She was disappointed when she spotted Edna sitting in the middle of a group of ladies waiting for the service to begin. Visiting with Edna would have to wait until the fellowship luncheon. Tootie waved and smiled a greeting to Edna and followed Hal and Nora to an empty place

After the worship service was over, the men set up the tables and the women went to the kitchen. Everyone had a job to make the preparations for the fellowship luncheon go smoothly and quickly. Before long, lunch was ready to serve the men, followed by the children and next the women.

When it was the women's turn to eat, Tootie filled her plate and searched for Edna Mast again. She was delighted when she saw plenty of room at Edna's table. Tootie set her plate down and asked, "May I sit by you, Edna?"

"Sure you can," said Edna, giving her a weak smile.

"It is so nice to see you again," Tootie declared, patting Edna's hand.

Edna said cheerfully, "It is nice to see you." As if someone pulled a roll down shade over her head, a blank look covered her face. She studied Tootie intently. "Do I know you?"

"I'm Nurse Hal's aunt. You surely remember me. I have visited John and Hallie Lapp several summers in a row. My name is Tootie."

Edna's smile widened. "Jah, now I do. How are you?"

"I'm just fine. How are you doing?" Tootie asked.

"I could be better. The aches and pains come with old age, ain't so? You know how it is. If one part is not ailing another part of the body is, and the aches keep circling around," Edna said. She turned her attention back to eating her food.

"We're going to be living here from now on so you and me will see each other often. We'll have plenty of time to visit," Tootie said.

Edna nodded. "That is nice." She studied Tootie while she

chewed a bite of ham. With a puzzled expression, she asked, "We will see each other again? Do I know you?"

"Yes, I'm Tootie. Nurse Hal's aunt," Tootie said slowly.

"Oh, that one," Edna said as if she wasn't impressed.

Margaret Yoder's warm smile caused her wrinkles to fan out at the corners of her mouth as she took a seat across from them. "Tootie, it is so nice to hear you folks will be living in our community. I like knowing we will have gute neighbors."

"Thank you," Tootie said, feeling a little better now that Margaret seemed happy to see her. At least Margaret was willing to talk to her, but she was one woman that could talk to anyone. She was raised Amish in Pennsylvania, married an Englisher and reverted back to being Amish. "We were spending so much time with Hal's family it only made sense to move here."

"Ach! That is much the better for the rest of us to have you to visit with," Margaret said as they watched Edna leave without another word.

Tootie had to ask. "Margaret, what has happened to Edna. One minute she seemed to know me and the next she had to ask me who I was."

Margaret nodded sadly. "Poor woman. She has been going down hill for some time. She has gotten to be such a fergesslich (forgetful) person. Do not take what she does personally. If her head was not fastened to her body, I guess she would forget it sometimes, too."

Tootie thought how much Edna acted like Peter Rogies. He had Alzheimer's, and she feared that was what was wrong with Edna. No turning back from that disease no matter how hard she prayed for her friend.

Once they arrived home, the men did the chores. The women sat down for a few minutes before they started supper. Nora and Tootie talked about what to make the two babies that would soon join the family. Both women liked to knit baby caps, sweaters and socks.

Knowing that Hal and Emma agreed gifts they made would be appreciated and treasured. Since Nora and Tootie had so much to do right now what with the moving, they suggested boughten gifts would do fine. Both the women could always use baby shampoo, cotton diapers and blankets.

Nora said, "It's too bad we don't know if you're having boys or girls. That affects the gift's color you know."

"It seems to me these days most women go get a test done to find out what the baby will be," Tootie added.

"Your guess is as good as ours at this point. We haven't had a test done," Hal shared.

A light bulb went on in Tootie's mind. "Nora, we can do the pencil and string test on them."

Hal frowned. "Oh, no, Aunt Tootie. I don't think that is a gute idea."

"What is this pencil and string test?" Emma asked.

"You shouldn't ask," Hal hissed.

Tootie sat on the couch beside Emma and patted her arm. "Never mind her, Emma. It's an old fashion way of finding out if you're going to have a boy or a girl."

"I see. How does it work?" Emma was curious.

"We aren't actually sure how it scientifically works, but we believe that because everything is planned by God, he gave us this little tool to determine the gender of a child. Nora and I have tried it on expectant mothers for years and seen it done by others. It is a very accurate test," Tootie explained.

"All we have to do is find a pencil, a needle and a two feet piece of thread," Nora added as if both women had agreed to the test. "Where can we find these things, Hallie?"

Hal looked helplessly at Emma.

Emma smiled. "Go get what they need, Hallie. What can it hurt?"

"All recht, go to the clinic so we can use the table in there. I'll round up what you need," Hal said with no enthusiasm in her voice.

When she came back, she handed the pencil, needle and thread to Tootie.

Tootie stuck the needle in the pencil eraser and handed it and the thread to Nora. "You're better at seeing how to thread a needle than I am."

The women sat at the table.

Hal asked, "Who's first?"

"I think we should try the test on you, Hallie. After all, you're going to have your baby first," Tootie said.

"All recht." Hal laid her hand on the table. She turned her hand with the back against the table so the palm was up.

Tootie stood up and held the string in both her hands as she placed the pencil directly over the wrist. The pencil moved in a lazy circle over Hal's arm. Next the pencil went back and forth from hand to elbow. After several sways, Tootie announced, "Hallie, you are diffidently having a boy."

"Good to know. We can make things in blue for Hallie," said Nora. "Now, Emma, it's your turn."

Emma glanced at Hal and winked as she laid her hand on the table palm up.

Hal winked back at her. Suddenly, she was eager to see what her mother and aunt had to say about Emma's pregnancy. Hal and Emma were both pretty sure this test would stump Tootie if Hal's doptone worked properly.

Tootie moved close to Emma and held the pencil over her wrist. The pencil started with a circle. The motion switched to swaying diagonal from the thumb in a line across the arm.

Nora gasped. "Tootie, look."

"I see." Tootie proclaimed excitedly, "Emma, you're going to have twins."

While she was talking, the pencil circled and enlarged the circle over a wide area. Tootie grimaced as she grabbed the pencil to keep it from moving. "So there you have the pencil test. You can take it or leave it."

"So if I am having twins are they boys or girls or one of each?" Emma asked excitedly.

Nora shrugged. "When the pencil shows twins it can't pick out the sex of the babies."

"That is too bad." Emma commiserated. "You still do not know what color to make the baby clothes."

"What did that last large circle tell you?" Hal asked. "I've never seen that happen before."

"Oh, that didn't mean anything," Tootie dismissed as she darted a hard look at Nora and jerked the needle out of the eraser. She handed the pencil and needle to Hal. "You can put these back where you got them."

Hal smiled at Emma. "You want to tell them how close they are to being recht with that test."

"Jah," Emma said. "Aendi Tootie and Mammi, Hallie did a doptone test on me. She heard two heartbeats. We are pretty sure I am having twins."

"See the test works," hooted Tootie.

Nora frowned. "Emma, you aren't still thinking about having these babies at home are you? The best place for you is at the hospital."

"That is what Hallie told me. Jah, I will go to the hospital when the time comes as bad as I wanted to be home for the delivery," Emma said.

Hal turned around at the clinic door. "There will be another time you can deliver at home. Have you made that appointment with Doctor Burns yet?"

"Nah, but I will tomorrow. I was waiting until I had school out of the way," Emma said.

Hal answered, "Gute."

It was hard for Hal to wait for Emma and Adam to go home that night. She had seen the sour looks pass between her mother and Tootie ever since they did their pencil test. She had an uneasy feeling there was something they didn't want to say in front of Emma.

So while they washed the supper dishes, Hal said, "Will one of you tell me what went wrong with Emma's pencil test? I know something did."

"It was probably a fluke. You shouldn't worry about it," Nora said offhandedly as she wiped off the table.

"Surely it was," Tootie agreed as she set a plate in the rinse pan. "Best to forget it, Hallie."

"Just the same if you two are worried so am I. I want to hear what the test showed," Hal insisted as she dried a plate.

Tootie glanced over her shoulder at Nora for an answer. She shrugged as she kept wiping the table. "Go ahead. Tell her."

Tootie put another plate in the rinse pan. "Hallie, when the pencil makes a large circle that's supposed to mean Emma is going to lose the baby. I sure didn't want to say that in front of her."

"Oh, fudge! I'm glad you didn't, but you might be recht," Hal said, looking worried.

"Why?" Nora asked as she put her dish cloth on the line behind the stove and came to Hal.

"I have to sit down a minute." Hal pulled a chair out at the table. She held her head in her hands as she told them what was worrying her. "When I listened to the babies heartbeats, one set of beats was very weak. I had the feeling one of the twins isn't doing gute, but I didn't have the heart to tell Emma. That's why I encouraged her to go to Doctor Burns. I know he'll have her do an ultrasound. That's the test you referred to Aunt Tootie. If something is wrong it will be his job to tell her so call me a coward if you must."

Nora and Tootie sat quickly beside Hal at the table.

"You did what was best for Emma by sending her to Doctor Burns. You're right. It is his job to explain what he finds to Emma and Adam," Tootie sympathized.

"Sounds like Emma needs prayers on her and her babies behalf. That much we can all do," Nora said. "Now you sit and rest, Hallie. Tootie and I can finish these dishes. You're in no shape to wait hand and foot on us and worry about Emma."

Chapter 5

Now that school was out Emma had spare time on her hands. For just Adam and her, it didn't take long to redd the house. Besides, it was much too quiet at home after all the time she spent with children studying and laughing as they played. She watched the clock. Close to noon on that sunny May morning, she drove to Adam's furniture shop with three lunches in a dish towel bundle.

"Gute Morgen, Priscilla. How has your morning been?" Emma greeted as the door bell tinkled her arrival.

Priscilla had her back to the door, rearranging Adam's handmade bird houses on the shelf behind the counter, She turned around, smiling from ear to ear. "Sure enough, this has been a gute morning. Adam will have to find time to replenish his bird house inventory. I sold six already this morning. The winter must have been hard on Englishers's old bird houses."

"That and word has gotten around that Adam makes bird houses that are different from the ones in the stores." Emma studied the row of miniature building structures. Adam meant to please a variety of birds for his English buyers. He had built rustic log cabins, red barns and yellow Victorian cottages. Larger brown chalets had three rooms for birds that didn't mind having neighbors. The plain boxes could be tacked to fence posts for bluebirds. Leaning against the counter end was the plain looking, two story, white houses, with several a dozen rooms built together for the purple martins. That bird was a favorite of Amish buyers. Those customers wouldn't consider the other birdhouses plain at all.

She laid her bundle on the counter. "I reckon the fact that Adam's houses are different is what sells them sure enough. The birdhouses are much sturdier than the store bought ones. They will survive many winters, and they are nice to look. Ain't so?

Now why I am here is to tell you I have brought lunch for you, Adam and me. I wondered if we could have a picnic in the timber?"

Priscilla shrugged. "Adam has been working on a project this morning in the workshop. He's the boss. You will have to ask him if he is willing to take time off."

"We have to eat, ain't so? Sure enough, if he will not stop, I will threaten to divide his lunch between me and you," Emma threatened.

Priscilla laughed. "That should convince him to say jah."

When Emma walked through the workshop door, Adam looked up from his jigsaw. He smiled as he nodded a greeting.

"I have brought dinner for the three of us. How about stopping long enough to eat with Priscilla and me?" Emma invited.

Adam stopped the jigsaw. He clapped his hands and rubbed his stomach before he took his pad and pencil out of his shirt pocket. He wrote, "I do not have much time. I am making cupboards for your mammi's kitchen. Did you make that call to Doctor Burns already?"

"Jah, I went earlier this morning to the phone shed to make an appointment for Wednesday afternoon. Now I want to go sit under the trees at the edge of the timber where it is cool and eat a picnic lunch. As soon as you eat, you can go back to work if you must," Emma said.

It was a short walk to the edge of the timber behind the shop, through a grassy area that stretched south to the trees. Emma tried to match her stride with slender, long legged Priscilla when she knew that was impossible. She waddled more like a duck these days. Adam stayed close to her in the unleveled terrain so he could catch her if she stubbed her toes.

Emma waved at a swarm of tiny buffalo gnats dancing in the air out of her way.

Adam batted at the air to keep the gnats away.

"Those gnats are thick right now," Priscilla complained.

"They sure hurt when they bite for as small as they are," Emma declared.

Priscilla rubbed the top of her head. "I hate the crawly feeling under my prayer cap when they crawl into my hair."

From where they stopped under a large hickory nut tree on the edge of the timber, Adam could see the shop if a customer came. After he helped Emma to the ground, she took three smaller bundles out of the large one and handed out two of them.

After they finished eating and put the napkins and towels back into the dish towel, Adam rubbed his stomach and smiled.

"Gute, it makes me happy that we could eat dinner together. That does not happen very often. I am glad you are full. Since I have buttered you up, I would like to explore the timber. I had been taking a shortcut through from the house when the school was in the shop's upstairs. I am having trouble seeing my feet recht now, but I would love to walk clear to the other end and back."

Adam had his note pad out, writing. "Sorry, too much work to take time off."

"I see. Suppose you could do without your sales clerk for a short time this afternoon? I am probably not safe to go by myself right now." Emma rubbed her expanding stomach.

Adam shrugged and wavered his hand at Priscilla.

"Sure, if you do not mind. I have taken plenty of walks through here so I know my way around," Priscilla said, crossing her long legs at the ankles.

"Gute. Just so we are not wasting our time, I brought a grocery sack for each of us. Maybe we will find mushrooms." Emma handed Priscilla a sack and stuffed Adam's sack inside hers. "Think you can eat fried mushrooms if I find some?" She asked Adam.

Adam's head bobbed up and down as he helped Emma up and made sure she was stable on her feet before he turned loose.

"You go back to work. We will not stay in the timber long," Emma said.

He waved good bye and headed for the shop.

"That husband of yours is sure a hard worker," Priscilla stated.

"I know. I wish he had more time for a little fun. That will come maybe when he gets my grossdawdi and mammi and Aendi Tootie's houses remodeled. Sure enough, we best get on with our walk so you can get back to work. You are on a bird house selling streak. I do not want to jinks that." Emma joked.

For few minutes, they walked through the trees and listened to the breeze rattle the new, crisp leaves over head. Priscilla said, "This timber is just about like any other, but it is not as big as the Bender Creek timber. There is one spot I think is special. Want to see it?"

"Stop!" Emma shouted. "Watch where you walk. Look!" Emma pointed in front of Priscilla's sensible black shoes.

"Sure enough, I best pay attention. Look at all the mushrooms peeking from under the dried leaves. Hold your sack open, and I'll pick them. I do not think it wise for you to bend over. You look too top heavy," Priscilla teased.

Emma giggled. "I not only look it. I am, and I keep reminding myself that will only get worse for the next three months."

Emma was so glad she suggested going for this walk with Priscilla. She hadn't always been nice to the young woman, but once they had gotten on better speaking terms, she saw what Bobby Keim found so likable about Priscilla. It was gute to have a friend that had similar interests.

As they walked on, Priscilla said, "Just ahead of us is what I want to show you." She pointed into a small clearing.

Emma's mouth fell open in awe when she saw the giant granite boulder split in half by a tree growing out of it. "That is really something, ain't so?"

"It sure enough is. That rock reminds me of a verse in the bible. *'Is not My word like fire?'*" declares the Lord. "'And *like a hammer which shatters a rock?'* Do you know that verse?"

"I do not," Emma admitted. "But it is probably one of those verses that did not make sense to me so I did not retain it. Now that I see this split rock and tree I can understand the verse. I will remember it now sure enough."

"This rock and tree reminds me how powerful God is. This is my quiet place to be alone to think and to be close to God. I come here when I can before or after work. Especially when I want to say a prayer for guidance or help. This clearing is such a peaceful place. So tranquil I feel God's presence here when I talk to him," Priscilla shared.

The corner of Emma's mouth twitched as she tried not to smile. "I see. Have you needed help with something as monumental lately as when God split this rock?"

"Not exactly help, just guidance," Priscilla answered, studiously rubbing the top of the rock to avoid looking at Emma.

"I see." Emma smiled. "Would your difficulty have anything to do with Bobby Keim?"

"Oh, but jah. It has everything to do with Bobby," Priscilla declared.

"Sure enough, keep right on praying here if it helps. You will come to a decision, and it will be the right one for you. I am sure of it," Emma said, patting Priscilla on the back.

Priscilla looked so worried. "I hope so and soon. Bobby is getting tired of waiting for me to make up my mind."

"Ach! I would not worry about Bobby. He is just impatient to hear you say jah, but he is not going to give up on you as long as he has hope. From what I saw at the shop between the two of you I can say he has plenty of hope," Emma teased.

Priscilla blushed so red it was as if she had a sunburn.

On Wednesday afternoon, Adam drove Emma to Doctor Burns's office in Wickenburg. Adam stayed in the waiting room while the doctor examined Emma.

"Hello, there Emma. My goodness it has been some time since I've seen you," the smiling, silver haired doctor greeted.

"Jah, some time," Emma agreed, ducking her head bashfully.

"I remember when you were only so high with a bad case of poison ivy," the doctor said. He measured four feet off the floor with his hand. "Now here you are a wife and soon to be mother. Times sure has a way of getting away from me when I realize I'm on my third generation of patients. In some cases, it is a fourth generation. How are those brothers and sisters of yours and the rest of the family," Doctor Burns asked as he sat on his stool by his computer.

"Noah and Daniel are fine, almost ready to be out on their own. Hallie does have her hands full with the two smaller girls. They are a handful yet." Emma relaxed as she shared.

"I expect they are from what I've seen of them." The doctor concentrated on Emma and got down to business. "What brought you in here?"

"When Nurse Hal used her doptone, she said she thought she heard two separate heartbeats. Maybe I am having twins. Hallie wanted you to check me to see for sure."

"Ah! Nurse Hal wants a second opinion, does she? You stretch out on the exam table so I can listen. Give me a few minutes, and I'll tell you what I find," Doctor Burns instructed as he winked at her.

After the exam, Emma straightened her clothes as the doctor called the nurse. He became solemn as he told his nurse to send Mrs. Keim's husband in.

Doctor Burns had been the go to expert for medical help in the Amish community long before Nurse Hal arrived. This warm hearted man, with salt and pepper hair, was loved by all his patients.

Emma felt something was wrong by how quickly Doctor Burns turned serious. She took Adam's hand and waited for the doctor's explanation, dreading what he had to say.

Looking over the rim of his gold reading glasses, Doctor Burns sat on his stool. "Nurse Hal was right to send you in for a checkup, Emma. You are having twins.

There's a problem with one of the twins. The baby's heart is weaker. If you both are agreeable I want to make an appointment at the hospital for an ultrasound right away. You can stop there on your way home. Ultrasound tests don't take

Priscilla's rock

"Is not My word like fire?" declares the Lord. "and like a hammer which shatters a rock?"

Jeremiah 23:29

long. The results are sent to me. On your way out, stop at the reception desk and make an appointment for Friday. We will discuss the findings that day."

Emma looked at Adam, and he nodded yes.

"That is gute with us, Doctor," Emma said as the nurse helped her off the exam table.

In about an hour and a half from the time the couple entered the hospital, the couple climbed into the buggy and headed home.

Normally, Emma took in the scenery they went by after they left town. They passed the tree nursery filled with plums and cherries full of bloom. She'd usually pointed out to Adam how pretty the trees were. This time she sat quietly staring at her hands in her lap while she thought about the test procedure. She hadn't heard any of the other Amish women talk about going through such a test. Why did she have to do it?

Finally, she said, "I feel there was something wrong with the babies. The woman who performed the ultrasound did not look happy."

Adam took his pad from his pocket and wrote, "She was just serious about doing a gute job."

"Sure enough, that must be so," Emma agreed and let the matter drop. Anything Adam said wouldn't keep her from worrying about her babies.

They stopped long enough at the Lapp farm for Emma to tell Hal they didn't have anything to report. They had to go back to Doctor Burns on Friday afternoon and hear the test results. She had an awful feeling something was wrong.

Hal told Emma to stop worrying. Taking an ultrasound was a procedure done on many women for various reasons.

Emma nodded. She understood, but her fears wouldn't calm until Doctor Burns talked to them Friday.

Thursday dragged by for Emma, and so did Friday morning. Once they arrived at the doctor's office, one of the nurses called Adam and Emma to come back to an exam room with her.

Not long after they were seated, Doctor Burns came in and pulled his wheeled stool over in front of them. He had the folded sonogram in his hands and a serious look on his face. "I have pictures here of your babies, a girl and a boy. Before I show them to you, it's my job to give you the bad news.

The girl looks fine. Growing at the normal rate and has a strong heartbeat. The boy has serious problems. The reason his heartbeats are weak is because he has a hole in his heart. That would take surgery to fix.

In most cases, if a baby with a bad heart lives through delivery, the surgery can be done. Not in this case. The boy has brain damage. He probably won't live once he is delivered. He might even die before delivery time. There's no medical procedure for fixing his under developed brain like we can his heart. That's why I think he won't live. I want you to look at these pictures. You can see from these that he's much smaller than his sister because he isn't thriving."

Doctor Burns handed the sonogram pictures to Emma. She unfolded them and handed the end to Adam so he could look with her.

Doctor Burns added, "I want you to notice the girl is taking special care of her brother. She's holding his hand so he knows he isn't alone. I've never seen that happen before. Usually, twins are batting at each other, trying to give themselves more room in the cramped uterus. I'd say that girl knows she is Amish already."

Tears formed in Emma's eyes as she said to Adam, "I take that as a sign from God. He has our daughter looking out for her brother."

Doctor Burns shook his head. "I agree."

Adam took out his pad and wrote, "It is comforting to know that our son is not alone at this time." He tilted the pad for Emma to read then handed it to Doctor Burns.

The doctor replied, "In a way, as a twin he's one lucky little baby to have such a caring sister with him right now when he needs her."

Emma took a deep breath so she could speak. "Do you think there is no hope at all for the boy?"

"It is my opinion that only a miracle can save him. I do recommend a cesarean section before you go into labor. We can control getting both babies into this world as fast as possible. They will be rushed into incubators with oxygen and the Neonatal department's special care. Your labor contractions would surely be more than the boy could stand."

Adam and Emma stopped by the Lapp farm with heavy hearts. It was hard to digest the news that they were going to lose one of their firstborns. It was even harder yet to speak of it out loud to the babies' grandparents, great grandparents and Tootie.

Adam went to the barn to talk to John, Jim and the boys while Emma went to the house.

She looked around. "Where are my little sisters?"

"Still taking a long nap," Hal said.

"That is gute. We should go in and sit down at the table. I wanted to talk to you three without them listening. This news would be hard for Redbird and Beth to understand." Once they sat down, Emma explained Doctor Burns findings, the women's eyes filled with tears at what was to happen to the boy twin.

Emma said, "You knew already that the news would not be gute, ain't so, Hallie?"

"Jah, I thought the one baby's heartbeats was weak. That's why I wanted you go see Doctor Burns." Hal pointed at her mother and aunt. "These two told me something was wrong. Remember when the pencil made that wide circle during the boy or girl test? They told me later that meant a miscarriage. I kept praying for once their pencil test would be wrong."

Nora took Emma's hand. "Is there no hope at all for the baby boy?"

"Doctor Burns said it would take a miracle for him to live past delivery. The hole in his heart could be fixed, but there is something wrong with his brain which cannot be fixed. We have to wait and see what happens," Emma told her.

"If it is a miracle it takes to save your baby, we're going to pray real hard for one," Tootie said.

"Jah, I will see that a prayer circle is started soon," Hal assured Emma.

"Tootie and I can help with that," Nora said. "I will call

our friends in Titonka and ask them to start a prayer circle until we tell them different."

"We have already had one miracle of sorts," Emma said. "Look at the sonogram pictures." She handed the pictures to Hal to unfold so Nora and Tootie could study, too. "Baby sister is holding baby brother's hand so he knows she is caring for him. He knows he is not alone and has her strength to fall back on all the time. Doctor Burns says that really surprised him since most twins are batting and kicking at each other in that tight space." Emma teared up. "The doctor says our baby girl knows she is Amish already to be so caring."

"Bless her tiny heart, and thanks to Doctor Burns for saying something so wonderful to Adam and you." Nora dabbed at her nose with her hanky as she sniffled.

Tootie stated,"Isn't that something? Her taking care of her brother is a miracle indeed."

"With that said maybe we will get an even better miracle for the baby boy," Hal said.

Chapter 6

So one of the days while Emma waited for her next visit with the doctor, she rode along with Adam to her dawdi and mammi's place. Hal and she helped Nora and Tootie set their houses in order. As Adam finished the closets and cupboards, the women emptied boxes to fill the areas up.

Nora and Tootie protested Emma should sit and rest. They didn't think she should be so active until the babies were brought into this world. Nora declared it was just nice to have her there to visit with them.

Emma assured the women she knew her limits, and she'd be careful until the delivery. Doctor Burns hadn't set the date yet so she couldn't sit and do nothing while she waited. Not being busy gave her more time to think and sorrow over what was likely to happen to her baby boy.

"That was understandable," Tootie commiserated.

Nora admonished, "Worry will get you no where, young lady. Use that time constructively with prayers for that miracle your baby needs."

Another day, Emma cleaned her house. When the danger of frost passed in the middle of May, she planted the garden space Adam cleared for her. She told herself she had to get caught up on her work while she felt like it. Besides, she had to be ready at a moment's notice to help Hallie deliver her baby. She wanted to spend some time with the latest Lapp addition to the family and make sure Hallie would be all right. Mammi and

Aendi Tootie said they would stick close to Hallie and take care of the family. With their help, Emma didn't feel bad about staying home most of the time to take care of herself.

She set up a corner of her bedroom with the baby cradle on a table. She placed a stack of diapers and powder next to the cradle. With a gentle rub over the cradle Adam so lovingly made, Emma wished she had talked him in to making another one for the baby boy. When she asked, her practical husband wrote they had to stay grounded in the fact Doctor Burns might be right about the baby dying. If with a miracle from God, the baby lives, then the cradle was large enough to hold two babies for a few days while he built another one. Bless Adam! He didn't want either one of them to get their hopes up.

On one Wednesday, Jim, John and the boys went to the Wickenburg salebarn. Jim hired a truck to deliver a buggy horse broke to plow and a Jersey cow that was going to freshen soon. Noah and Daniel patched the chicken house to hold the two dozen red hens and one black and red araucana rooster.

Jim declared their new place sounded like a real country home with a rooster crowing to wake them up. The horse whinnying, and the cow bellering for feed was an added bonus for Jim. Always, they could depend on the hens, when they scattered over the yard, to cackle at their shadows if nothing else.

*   *   *

Finally by the first of June, Emma worked herself out of keeping busy jobs. One afternoon she cut through the timber to the furniture shop to visit with Priscilla. Adam would scold her for not driving over if he found out. If he did, she'd tell him she needed the exercise.

She couldn't help but be curious how close Priscilla was to becoming Adam's sister-in-law. By now she hoped to find out encouraging news. News that was happy for a change. If not, she could offer more advice to Priscilla to urge her into making up her mind.

At the far side of the timber, she stopped at the edge of the grass. From there she heard the bell tinkle when the shop door opened. It surprised Emma to see Albert Jostle, a tall nineteen year old neighbor, come outside. He pulled his right suspender off his arm and up on his shoulder. Hitching up his pants as if he was going to lose them, Albert trotted down the driveway to the road. He looked both ways and raced for home like he had a gaggle of angry geese after him.

What was wrong with Albert? He was acting sneaky, but when wasn't he odd? The sullen young man rarely spoke to anyone at worship services. Why was he at the shop? His family was poor. He certainly couldn't afford to buy Adam's fine, handcrafted furniture.

She continued through the meadow, watching to avoid the bumble bees buzzing over the yellow dandelion blooms, resembling pats of butter scattered in the grass. It wouldn't be a good thing to step on a bee while barefoot or to have a bee fly up her dress and sting her while he tried to find a way out.

She opened the shop door. The bell jingled. "Hello, Priscilla, are you busy?"

There wasn't an answer. Emma walked across to the workshop door. She opened it. "Adam?"

No answer. That was strange. She knew Adam was probably gone on a job since he was still working at her grandparents place, but Priscilla should be here working today.

Emma tried to figure out where the store clerk went as she looked around. The shelf behind the counter that held the bird houses was a mess. Some of the houses were turned over, and others on the verge of falling off. How could that have happened? Priscilla had the houses so neatly displayed.

Emma walked around the end of the counter to straighten up the shelf. She froze when she heard a moan and looked down. It was Priscilla curled up in a ball on the floor with a white pillow case over her head. She wasn't moving. Painful moans escaped the cotton case. Her dress front was ripped wide open, exposing her breasts. Straight pins glimmered on the dress and were scattered on the floor. Priscilla's underpants were wadded in a ball under the counter, and one untied shoe lay on its side below Priscilla's feet. A pool of blood oozed from under the woman's legs, ran along her calves and darkened her black socks past the knees. Another dark, irregular shaped stain spread across her navy blue skirt.

Emma eased to her knees beside Priscilla and pulled the pillow case off her head. She grabbed the woman's shoulders to place her onto her back. Priscilla opened one blackened eye and shrank away when she felt Emma's touch. She screamed a piercing howl and then wailed.

Emma tried to calm her. It was almost more than she could bear to look at the poor woman. Her face had been badly beaten. One eye puffy black, and the other swollen shut. Her lips were bloated, and the bottom lip was split. Blood colored a cut on the side of her swollen left cheek. No doubt about it. Priscilla had put up a hard fight with someone.

"This is so awful. Who did this to you?" Her friend's dark eyes stared blankly ahead as if she couldn't see or hear Emma. "Priscilla, can you hear me?"

Priscilla doubled up, grabbed her stomach and responded with a groan. The woman needed an ambulance. Priscilla was badly hurt from an assault and losing too much blood. She was probably already in shock.

"Priscilla, I am going for help. I will not be long. Just stay still until I get back." Emma rushed out the door and climbed into Priscilla's buggy. She ran the horse to the phone shed just past her house at the end of the mile. With a trembling finger, she poked the numbers 911 and explained what happened. She said to tell the hospital ER they need to have a rape evidence kit ready when the victim arrived. Next call she made was to Sheriff Dawson. He said he'd be right out.

Emma drove back to the shop and rushed inside. "Priscilla, I am back." She came to a sudden stop when she reached the counter. All she found was a bloody outline on the floor where Priscilla had been.

Sirens told her help was close so she waited outside, not wanting to spend any time in the shop until she knew Priscilla was all right.

The ambulance drove in with the sheriff's car right behind it. Emma told the three EMTs, Daryl, Steve and Ivan, and the sheriff as calmly as she could what happened, and that the patient had disappeared.

Sheriff Dawson said he'd get on his car radio and call for a search party to help. Just having the tall, neatly dressed man, in his official tan uniform, take charge made Emma feel better.

Daryl, Steve and Ivan shook their heads in agreement with the sheriff.

Daryl said, "If the woman has lost so much blood and is still bleeding, we need to find her fast."

As the sheriff headed to his car, Emma agreed. "She was too hurt to get far. If you look at the amount of blood behind the counter, you can see how badly she is bleeding. As for confused, she is in such pain she is out of her head. She was fighting me off when I tried to help her as if I was the attacker. I think I might know where Priscilla has gone."

The sheriff turned back to her. "We can always call for a search party if we don't find her. You lead the way, Mrs. Keim."

The ambulance personnel followed, carrying a stretcher. Emma led them across the grassy strip and into the timber. She prayed they would find Priscilla soon and that the young woman was still alive when they found her.

Hopefully, Priscilla was at the rock, thinking that was where she'd be safe. The rock had always given her peace and consolation.

The leaves on the trees whispered to her overhead, making Emma wonder if that was God's sign to calm her worries for Priscilla. Was he trying to tell her she was headed the right direction? She sure hoped so.

When they got to the clearing, Emma breathed a sigh of relief. Priscilla huddled against the rock, but she was so very still, Emma bit her lower lip and prayed that the woman was still alive.

EMT Daryl touched Priscilla's shoulder and said her name softly.

She came unglued when she opened her eyes and saw the strange man standing over her. She shrank away from him, lashing out with her fists as she screamed, "Don't touch me."

Emma stepped forward, wanting to help.

Daryl put his arm out to keep her away. "Stay at a safe distance. You don't want her to hit you."

Emma nodded to show she understood. "Priscilla, please be calm. These men are here to help you. They are from the hospital. You need to go with them. You are hurt."

Priscilla quieted as if she understood. She gave Emma a dazed stare when she recognized her friend's voice, trying to comprehend what Emma said.

Emma held out her hand. Priscilla took it and braced her back against the rock to as she stood. Steve and Ivan reached out and helped steady the woman when her knees buckled. They turned her sideways and laid her gently on the stretcher. She flattened out and let Daryl cover her up with a blanket.

Emma had to walk fast to keep up with the EMTs as they carried Priscilla through the timber. Sheriff Dawson tried to slow her pace. "Take it easy. You don't want to fall."

"Denki, but I want to be with my friend."

"I understand," the sheriff said.

The fast walk left her breathless when she stopped to watch Priscilla rolled inside the ambulance. "Priscilla is my friend and works in my husband's furniture shop. She will not be able to answer your questions. Can I go along to give you the information you need?"

"Sure, Priscilla might feel less anxious with a friend with her," Daryl said. He helped Emma into the ambulance to sit on one of the benches beside the gurney.

Emma leaned over Priscilla. "I am going to the hospital with you." When Priscilla didn't answer, she gave Daryl a concerned look.

Daryl said, "Relax, Emma. Her vitals are fine. She just doesn't have it in her to respond right now."

Emma leaned back to wait out the bumpy ride. *So this is what it is like to ride in an ambulance. Sure enough, I hope Adam finds my note on the shop counter. I will need a ride home later. Now, God, I am praying for your help to heal Priscilla and to ask that you do not let my babies come too soon from this ambulance's rough bouncing.*

In such close quarters, Emma felt as if they were soaring as the ambulance sped toward the hospital. The bouncing and speeding motions made her queasy. She'd been over morning sickness for a couple months, but riding in this ambulance was bringing the urpy feeling back. She wished she knew how close they were to the emergency room at the hospital. The sooner she could get out and breathe fresh air the better she would feel. Wrapping her arms around her middle, she tried to keep her lunch in her stomach.

In the cab, Emma heard a static radio voice ask for estimated arrival time. Steve answered, "Five minutes. We are almost to Wickenburg city limits."

Daryl glanced up from tending his patient. "Emma, are you all right? You look a little green around the gills?"

Emma nodded. "Has anyone ever complained about being sea sick in an ambulance?"

Daryl laughed. "Not that I remember, but there's always a first time for everything."

Chapter 7

That same morning, Hal set the wicker laundry basket full of dampened clothes rolled in balls on the table. She went back to the mudroom and carried the ironing board with the gray cover and scratched legs over by the table.

When she opened the legs, the screech of metal against metal sounded similar to the screech owl that often made its mating calls outside her bedroom window. In the middle of the night, the owl's unearthly screams made Hal bolt straight up in bed. Either sound, ironing board or owl, set her teeth on edge.

She placed the sad irons on the cookstove to heat. The girls were playing nurse and patient in the clinic. Hal thought she had time to rest and have a cup of tea. She'd just collapsed in a chair and took a sip when she heard Gano bawl in the barn. Her two kids and two orphan lambs joined in with the chorus.

Hal glanced at the irons about ready to use, heating on the stove. She looked toward the kitchen window, listening to the din in the barn. She mumbled to herself, "Gano, couldn't you give it a rest for once and become a responsible mother? You no sooner hop over that pen and your babies miss you."

The irons had to be hot by now. That bothersome goat could care less that Hal had work to do. If she didn't want to listen to the ruckus in the barn for the rest of the day, she had to take the time to go check on the goat. She knew what was wrong. Like usual Gano had hopped out of the pen. The babies missed her and were hungry. They wanted her back in with them.

When Hal stepped out on the porch, she realized the day was pleasant enough. As hot as she was, the gentle breeze felt good and was just strong enough to cause the windmill blades to squeak disagreeably. While Hal walked down the porch steps, she wished she felt like working in the garden this afternoon. It was a wish that wasn't going to happen. By the time she stood on her feet ironing and cooked lunch, she knew she'd be done in.

John and the boys went for the day to help build a new machine shed at Luke Yoder's farm. The shed would replace the machine shed that was damaged by the tornado. Her parents and Tootie were working at their place until late afternoon, so she didn't have to fix much lunch for herself and the girls. They could eat leftovers from last night's supper.

Hal opened the top half of the barn door and peeked in. The hinges squeaked. Gano recognized the sounds and came to meet her. Joseph, the rooster, was scratching through some loose hay in the corner. He crowed a greeting.

"Joseph! What are you doing in the barn? You should be out with the hens. Some father you're going to make. If you keep hanging out with this incorrigible goat, you will never get to be a father. That means I won't have fryers to butcher in the fall," Hal scolded. The rooster stretched his neck out at the sound of her voice. Hal pointed at the goat. "You should pick better friends. You're letting that bad example of a mother rub off on you."

Hal unwound the wire holding a metal gate against the end of the pens. She flapped her apron tail at the goat. Gano turned and trotted back down the walkway between the pens. Quickly, Hal scooted the gate across the opening. She'd get Joseph shooed out of the barn door and open the pen door to let Gano into her babies like always.

She flapped her apron at Joseph and headed him toward the door. The rooster saw the top half open and flew up to perch on it. He wavered back and forth as he gave a lusty crow and flew out into a flock of hens, causing them to squawk in surprise.

Hal turned around in time to see Gano on the run toward the gate, wanting very much to join her rooster friend. Hal flapped her apron at the goat and yelled for her to stay put. Gano had a mind of her own and seldom paid any attention to Hal. She jumped but wedged one of her back legs in the top of the metal gate just as Hal got close. The gate fell toward Hal. The top of it landed on her left foot. She hit the floor hard and groaned in pain. Determined to look for Joseph, Gano bawled as she walked across the gate, adding her weight to Hal's injured foot.

Hal grunted as she pushed the gate off her foot. The outside ankle and top of the foot instantly swelled and colored black. She was afraid the ankle bone broke. No way did she want to stand on her foot as painful as it felt to see if it would hold her weight.

She hadn't bothered to tell her daughters when she left the house. Hopefully, the girls would miss her soon. She should have told them she was going to the barn, but she thought she'd be right back.

She pushed backward with her hands until she had scooted against the pen wall. Maybe if she sat there for a while the pain in her foot would decrease. She closed her eyes, clamped her lips together and prayed for God to help her out of this mess.

Hal didn't know how much time passed before she heard Redbird's shrill voice calling for her. Her eyes popped open. She yelled, "Redbird, come here. I'm in the barn."

A cramp hit her in the midsection. She groaned as she held her stomach with both hands. Nah, this can't happen. It's too soon for the baby to come. She said loudly, "Redbird, can you hear me?"

"Jah, I hear," the girl answered.

"We coming," Beth added.

The two girls chattered about something as they walked to the barn. Thank goodness she'd left the bottom door unhooked. The girls weren't tall enough to reach over to unhook it.

The girls clambered into the barn. They ran over to Hal and knelt beside her.

Redbird took her hand. "Why are you sitting here?"

Beth placed her hands over her ears and made a face. "Gano is making such a racket and her babies, too."

"I know, but I hurt my ankle when the gate fell over on it. I can't get up to put her in her pen with her babies so they will all be quiet," Hal explained.

"We can do it." Redbird jumped up. "Come on, Beth."

The little girls stepped lightly over the gate and ran down the walkway to open the pen. Gano walked right in for them, acting like she missed her babies. She stood still and let the lambs and kids fight for a taste of milk.

Redbird told Hal, "Gano is penned up now. You coming to the house now?"

"I can't walk on my foot. Girls, do you know where I keep my nurse's bag in the clinic cupboard?"

Redbird said, "Jah."

Beth's head bobbed up and down in agreement.

"I want you to go back to the house. Climb on a chair so you can get to my bag. Please be careful not to fall off the chair. Only one injury at a time is allowed in this family. I'm it today. Find the cell phone in my bag and bring it to me," Hal instructed.

"Why?" Redbird asked.

"I have to call a doctor about my foot." Hal said through her teeth, trying not to grimace as another cramp came. It didn't last long. She let out the breath she'd been holding. "Bring me paper and a pen, too. I need to leave your daed a note so he knows we went to the doctor."

The girls raced away. They weren't gone too long. Redbird handed the cell phone to her mother. Hal worried the battery might be too weak. She hadn't had a reason to check it lately.

She turned the phone on and saw there was just enough energy left in the battery to make a short call. She paused long enough to thank God for small favors and dialed 911. When the dispatcher answered, she told the woman she needed an ambulance and why.

The wait for help seemed long. She now knew how her patients felt. She wasn't used to being the one taken to the hospital. The last time was when she had the car accident before she married John. When that happened she was unconscious so she didn't remember the ride.

Finally, the ambulance's siren wailed its arrival. "Girls, open the barn door and wave at the EMTs so they know where we are."

In seconds, she heard the back doors of the ambulance open and the chattering gurney wheels roll over the rough ground. Daryl was the first in the door with Steve and Ivan following behind.

"Hi, Hal. Fancy meeting you here in the barn. What happened?" Daryl asked, kneeling beside her.

"I fell when the milk goat knocked over that metal gate on my foot. I might have broken this ankle and or arch." Hal pointed at her bruised, swollen left foot.

"Whoa! That foot sure looks angry," Steve said as Daryl took vitals.

Daryl relayed the vitals while Ivan wrote them on a clipboard. Their attention was on Hal when she grabbed her midsection and groaned.

Daryl frowned. "Friend, looks like you have got more going on at the moment besides a badly hurt foot. How far along are you?"

"I've got another three weeks to go, but I don't feel like I'll make it that far," Hal grunted with both hands on her stomach.

"We'll help you get on the gurney and get you to the hospital fast," Daryl said.

"Fine, but we have to take my daughters with us. There's no one else home to take care of them," Hal told him. "Could one of you put this note on the kitchen table so John knows where I am?"

"Okay, we'll do that for you," Ivan said as he took off for the house.

"Now scoot over on the gurney," Daryl said as Steve leaned across the gurney and lifted while Daryl worked from the other side. With Hal's help they soon had her down and covered.

"You two girls want to go for a ride with your mother in our ambulance? I can put the siren on for you," Daryl said.

They stared at him, not knowing what to say.

Hal motioned for them to come to her. "It will be all recht. We're all going. I have to see a doctor about my hurt foot, and I need you to go along and take care of me."

Redbird gave Daryl a serious look. "We will go with you."

"Your mama has two very nice, big girls," Daryl praised.

Redbird and Beth said in unison, "Denki."

The girls followed the men out of the barn, holding on to each other as they watched their mother rolled into the ambulance. Steve motioned for them to come toward him. "Now let me lift you, girls. You can sit on one of the side seats by your mother."

Steve and Daryl climbed in the back to be with Hal while Ivan drove. The siren screamed as the men took Hal's vitals and asked her questions about her condition. The girls covered their ears with their hands at the sound of the loud siren. They didn't mind the fast ride on the gravel road, but they grew wide eyed as they felt the ambulance bounce over each joint in the pavement.

At the hospital, the EMTs brought Hal out of the ambulance and headed for the ER doors. Ivan followed, holding hands with the girls. The doors swooshed open. The men stopped long enough to find out which exam room to put Hal in. Lucy Stineford was the day charge nurse. She smiled at the girls and asked the men if they weren't hiring emergency personnel a little young these days.

*　*　*

By the time Emma arrived at the hospital with Priscilla, she did a double take when she saw John and the boys in the waiting room. Her sisters were asleep curled in chairs. She stopped long enough to find out what had happened and told them why she was there.

John told her he'd been in to see Hal briefly, but Doctor Christensen gave her something to make her doze. John decided to come back to the waiting room to sit with his children. They waited for the results of the foot x-rays to come back.

Hal would be in the hospital at least one night for observation because she was having cramps. John worried she might go into labor, and lose the baby.

Emma assured him, Hal was so close to her delivery date the baby should be fine, if there wasn't any injury from Hal's fall.

Adam found the note Emma left at the shop and drove to the hospital. He walked past the nurse's station and saw through the glass John and his family was in the waiting room. Sheriff Dawson stood in the hall talking to Emma. When he walked up behind his wife, he could tell she was being interviewed by the sheriff.

Dawson said, "I wanted to talk to Priscilla, but the nurse says she's too upset to talk. I can understand that so I will talk to her tomorrow. Now what can you tell me?"

Emma said, "I am not going to be much help. All I saw was Albert Jostle coming out of the shop in a hurry."

"Well, that's a place to start," said the lawman. "Seems like his name crops up often lately in your neighborhood."

"Jah, it does," Emma agreed, remembering how sure they all were that Albert was the barn burner. They were wrong that time. A bad feeling nagged at her now. Perhaps, she shouldn't have mentioned Albert to the sheriff this time.

"Evening, Adam," the sheriff said.

Emma turned around and leaned against him. "I am so glad to see you. I hoped you would find my note."

"Well, people, it is like this, I can't do much unless I have more to go on. I have to talk to Priscilla. If she confides in you, Mrs. Keim, will you ask her about what happened and let me know?"

"Sure enough, I will try," Emma said.

"If I can't see her tomorrow, I'll be out to the Tefertiller farm to question her myself very soon. You can tell her that," the sheriff said.

"All recht, I will tell Priscilla when she is up to listening," Emma told him.

It was then that Sheriff Dawson gave Adam and her some

dire warnings to pass on to the rest of the Amish community. Warnings, the Keims decided to relay to John Lapp. He could ask the bishop to bring the matter up at the next worship service announcement.

After the sheriff left, Adam pointed toward the waiting room full of Lapps. Emma told him what happened to Hal. She wanted to stay at the hospital with her family until Hallie was out of the woods.

Adam went into the waiting room to talk to Noah and Daniel. He took them back to the farm to milk. After he dropped the boys off, he drove over to the Lindstrom place to relay what had happened to Hal and Priscilla. After that, he came back to the Lapp farm to help do the chores.

Hal's parents and Tootie drove to the Lapp farm in the car. Jim helped with milking while Nora and Tootie fixed a bite to eat. After supper, Jim asked Adam if he'd like to ride with them to the hospital. Maybe Emma would be ready to come home.

Adam wrote, "That is a gute idea."

Throughout the evening, Hal continued to have contractions. As the pains came closer together and more severe, it was clear she was going to have the baby. The family left John with her and adjourned to the waiting room. As the evening hours passed, Emma declared everyone should go home and get a good night's sleep. Hal was getting good care. She and John would stay to deliver news when there was any.

John said, "Emma, you need your rest. You should go home, too."

"Nah, I was supposed to help Hallie with her delivery, but I am getting cheated out of it, because of her ornery goat. Sitting up with her is the least I can do," Emma insisted.

The next morning, Hal went into labor. As she was wheeled to the delivery room, John and Emma went to the cafeteria for breakfast. After that, they waited for news in the obstetrics waiting room.

It was mid morning when the doctor came through a set of double doors in his blue paper cap and gown. As he walked toward John and Emma, his shoes, covered with paper slippers, whispered.

John and Emma stood.

"Relax, both mother and baby are doing fine. Mr. Lapp you have a boy. He's healthy and weighed in at six pounds three ounces. We want to keep him three days to observe him for any problems from your wife's fall.

Your wife is being moved to the recovery room now. It won't be long until she's in a room. You can visit her then. Right now, would you like to go to the nursery? You can look through the window at your baby."

"Jah," John said.

"Good. I will send a nurse here to take you." The doctor turned and disappeared down the hall.

John muttered to Emma. "I was going to ask him how long Hal will have to stay. It seemed like an eawichkeit (eternity) until the doctor came. You never seen anyone get finished talking and disappear as quick as he did."

"Daed, he has lots of patients to take care of besides Hallie," Emma chided.

The nurse led the way and pointed to the baby in the incubator near the front window. "That one is baby Lapp."

"Oh, Daed," Emma gasped. "He looks small."

"I know, but the doctor said he is healthy. That is voonderball gute." John's voice held relief.

"My brothers and me look that small?" Emma asked.

"Jah, you did," John said.

Emma smiled. "Did you notice he looks like you? No red hair on this baby."

"Jah, I see. He is very much a Lapp," said John, grinning proudly at the baby.

The nurse said, "Mrs. Lapp is in her room now. I'll show you where she is."

They followed her down a long hallway to Hal's room. Hal was pretty groggy, but she attempted to smile. John took one hand and Emma took the other.

"We must look like something the cat drug in. We have had a long night," Emma explained.

"Jah, tell me about it. You should have been in my place, but I wouldn't wish a broken foot and birthing at the same time on anyone," Hal quipped.

"How is the foot?" Emma asked.

"Painful and the cast feels as if it weighs a ton." Hal teared up.

John decided it was time to change the subject. "We got to see the baby."

"I just held him for a few minutes, but I think he looks like Daniel. Don't you?" Hal asked.

"Emma and I figure sure enough that baby is a Lapp," John said proudly.

Emma felt like she could use some rest. Now that she knew Hal and the baby were all right, she was ready to go home and crawl into bed. "Hallie, I am going to leave Daed to watch out for you and go home."

"That is a gute idea. You look all done in. You need to get more rest than you have been lately," Hal cautioned.

After Emma left, John said, "We have to come up with a name for our baby son. Everyone will want to know."

Hal nodded. "I have been thinking about that. I'd like to name the baby after two of my favorite men. How about John James?"

John squeezed her hand. "I'd be proud for my son to have my name and that was the name of my father so we are including both grandparents."

"I will let you be the one to tell everyone," Hal said through a yawn.

Chapter 8

Hal and the baby had been home two days when Bishop Bontrager and Jane came to visit. Redbird and Beth were sitting quietly by the baby's cradle, watching him sleep. Biscuit's company bark sounded from the driveway. Nora and Tootie came from the kitchen to greet them at the door.

The Bontragers looked concerned as they studied Hal on the couch with her leg up on a pillow.

"Mom, could you bring two chairs from the table so Elton and Jane can sit by me?" Hal asked.

"It would be a shame to interrupt two busy women at work. I will go get our chairs," Elton offered.

As he placed the chairs by the couch, Jane said, "Redbird and Beth, how are you getting along with the baby?"

Redbird put a finger to her lips. "We are supposed to be quiet when he sleeps."

"We help Mama take care of him," Beth offered.

"I couldn't ask for two better helpers than my girls," Hal bragged.

"It is gute to have such gute help," Elton said, patting the girls on the head.

"We will try to be quiet like we are supposed to be," Jane told the girls.

Jane told Hal she looked good considering all she'd been through.

"I don't feel so bad, but it's hard to get my strength back

when I can't do much. I'm tethered to this couch by that cast on my leg," Hal complained.

"How long do you think the cast will be on?" Elton asked.

"Maybe two months. Denki to my mother and Aunt Tootie for being here to help me until I'm on my feet," Hal said.

Jane leaned down to look at the sleeping baby in the cradle beside the couch. "He is a sweet one sure enough."

"Jah, John James Lapp seems to be taking off well. He's healthy even though Gano caused him to come early. Praise the Lord," Hal said.

"Praise the Lord," the Bontragers said together.

"It is gute to have the baby home with you," Jane said.

"Jah, that keeps your mind occupied," Elton agreed. "Babies take much of a mother's time."

Hal whispered, "I'd agree if I could only keep his grandmother and aunt from stealing him away. I'm perfectly able to pick the baby up. I can diaper him and feed him recht here, but the second the baby squeaks, Mom and Aunt Tootie come running."

"Ach! That most new mothers had such a problem," Jane mocked, causing Elton and Hal to laugh.

"What are the men doing this morning?" Elton asked.

"They went to the barn for morning chores like usual. I heard the generator shut down about half an hour ago. I've been wondering myself what's keeping them," Hal said.

"I should just walk to the barn once and find out," Elton said.

Nora was standing in the kitchen door. "Good, tell them the coffee pot is on."

After the bishop left, the baby fuzzed and wiggled. Hal said, "I believe he's wet. Girls, can you get me a diaper, a wet wash cloth and the powder?"

The girls shot off the floor and ran for the baby supplies on the clinic table.

Jane leaned forward and spoke quietly, "When John stopped to tell us about you and the baby he told us what happened to Joseph Tefertiller's Priscilla. We saw the ambulance go by and wondered who was on the way to the hospital. That was such a horrible thing done to that poor girl."

"It certainly was. A man that attacks a woman like that has to be ferricked (deranged)," Hal agreed.

"Jah, but we did not get the details from John. He was too excited to tell us he was a father again sooner than you thought, and you were all recht after you tangled with the goat. Do you know what happened to Priscilla exactly," Jane said.

Hal repeated what Emma told her. "Priscilla was released from the hospital about the same time I was. Emma says the girl fought hard. Her face was badly battered from the beating the man gave her. Before they left the hospital, Emma asked Polly Tefertiller if she could see Priscilla. Polly said Priscilla doesn't want anyone around. This is going to be hard for the poor girl to get over."

"As it would be for any woman. I feel so sorry for her. We must all pray for her recovery," Jane said.

They stopped talking when Redbird came back with the diaper. Beth handed her mother the powder container and raced to the kitchen with a wash cloth in her hand. Hal spread the baby's blanket on her lap. By the time, she took off his diaper, Beth was back with a warm washcloth. Hal washed the baby, powdered his bottom and and put on the clean diaper. That didn't help. The baby whimpered. Hal opened the front of her dress and let the baby nurse.

"Denki for helping me, girls. Would you like to go to the barn and see how close to done the men are with chores?" Hal asked.

"Jah," the girls said in unison as they raced to the door.

Hal smiled. "They were more than eager to get outside, ain't so? They can only sit still so long to watch over the baby.

I think what happened to Priscilla Tefertiller is too much for them to digest recht now."

Jane nodded. "I agree."

"Now about Priscilla, she needs spiritual guidance from our bishop as well," Hal suggested.

"Sure enough, Elton and I will make a visit soon," Jane offered.

"Just keep in mind, Priscilla might not talk to you recht

away. If not you can just visit with her parents. That will be gute for them at least. As soon as I can get around, I want to go see how she is if she will see me as a nurse. Once I get her confidence then I can help with her mental status."

"Gute idea," Jane said.

Hal shared, "Priscilla had been keeping company with Bobby Keim. They talked about marriage. She won't see Bobby now, or anyone else for that matter. I hope this terrible incident doesn't ruin that couple's plans."

"So do I. We have to hope God has a plan and will make life better for all involved. Now how about we pick a happier subject while we are alone. Your little girls have a birthday coming soon, ain't so?" Jane asked.

"Jah. It's hard to believe they will be four years old in a few days. Mom and Aunt Tootie are going to bake them each a cake. John is making ice cream. Noah and Daniel will take turns helping John crank the freezer. You and Elton want to come to a very small birthday party?"

"We would be glad to come. I want every chance I can get to hold your new baby," Jane said.

Hal handed Johnnie to Jane. "Be my guest recht now. With his belly full he should be gute for you." Thinking about Emma, Hal's expression turned downhearted. "Enjoying the new baby and a birthday party is what this family needs to cheer us up recht now."

Jane frowned. "You do not sound cheerful. There must be something more I do not know. Was ist letz?"

"It's not something the matter with me. We're worried about Emma and Adam. I'd say by now it's no secret the Keims are expecting a baby.

Emma found out from Doctor Burns she's having twins, a girl and a boy." Hal held her hand up. "Don't look so happy, Jane. Normally, we'd all be tickled to hear the news, but the boy baby is not expected to live. He has a hole in his heart, and the doctor says brain damage. He is much smaller than the girl. It's clear he isn't thriving."

"Ach! What sad news. I will start a prayer circle for the Keims and their baby boy. You must have unwavering faith.

Perhaps, the doctor cannot be so sure what will happen. Maybe the baby will be fine with our voices raised in prayer," Jane encouraged. "Elton and I will go to the phone shed and make calls to everyone we know. We will make this one of the biggest prayer circles you have ever seen in all the communities. Elton can put an ad for prayers needed for Adam and Emma in the Budget. That magazine's circulation covers a wide area."

"Denki for your help," Hal said. "Mom and Aunt Tootie have a prayer circle going back home in Titonka, too."

"Gute, and while you are sitting here you could start a circle letter to ask for prayers," Jane said. "It would give you something to do."

"I guess I missed that in Aunt Tootie's book on Amish Customs. What is a circle letter?" Hal asked.

"Simple, this letter is for people that do not live close and have not heard the news about Adam and Emma's baby. You can ask them to pray for the the parents and the baby. Usually, the letter you write is full of family news, and what is going on in the neighborhood like the new school open house. You make a list of people and their addresses to be in the circle letter. Send your letter to the first person on the list. That person will write a letter like yours with the news in their neighborhood and send to the next person on the list along with your letter. After the letters have been sent to everyone on the list, the letters will come back to you. You take out your old letter and write a new letter. Send it again to the first person on the list. In the letter, you might ask all those in the circle to send a letter to many others to pray for the Keims."

"Sure, I can give it a try," Hal agreed.

Tootie said from the doorway, "In the old days we used to call that a chain letter, asking for recipes or sending hankies."

"That's recht, Aunt Tootie, we did," Hal agreed.

Elton came in. He looked from his wife's gloomy face to Hal's doleful face, but he didn't question them. He announced, "The men will be here soon."

"What was keeping them?" Hal asked.

"Yesterday John weaned the babies your goat was feeding.

This morning she needed milked. Each of the men took a turn. She would not stand still for any of them. Kept sticking her foot in the bucket and kicking at their hands. Hopped up and down in between the kicking."

"I've milked Gano a few times just to get her used to it. She was fine for me," Hal said puzzled.

"Maybe so, but the men gave up," Elton said. "They will be here as soon as they convince the goat to stay in her pen."

Hal grunted. "I hope they know something I don't. I haven't had any luck keeping that goat penned up."

When John, Jim and the boys walked through the door, they had the most nonplussed look on their faces.

Hal said, "I'm sorry Gano gave all of you such a hard time."

John ducked his head sheepishly. "Ach! That is one stubborn goat you bought from Rudy Briskey."

Hal slowly eyed each of them. "Where did you leave Redbird and Beth? I thought they were with you."

Daniel grinned. "They are bringing in the milk."

Elton exclaimed, "You finally got the goat to stand still. I just told Hal you did not have any luck."

Noah said sheepishly, "You were recht about us. We could not milk that goat, but the girls thought they could milk her."

"I'm sorry you had so much trouble. That big goat is a little too feisty for those small girls. Did they try to milk?" Hal asked.

"Sure, Redbird and Beth stood back and watched us struggle with that ornery goat forever," Jim exclaimed. "After we finally gave up and headed for the door, I turned about to see if they were coming with us. Redbird picked up the milk bucket, nodded toward the goat pen at Beth and headed down the alley. I got John and the boys' attention so we could watch.

Beth and Redbird went in the pen and put their arms around the goat's neck. They backed that goat up in a corner of the pen. Beth held her, rubbing her neck and talking to her quiet like while Redbird put the bucket under her and got on her knees. She butted her head into that goat's side and started milking. Beats any sight I ever saw before out of two small girls."

John smiled. "Those two are a lot like their mother."

"If they are that pleases me," Hal responded.

Nora scolded sharply, "You men left those two little girls out there alone with that ornery goat after you upset the animal?"

Jim shrugged. "They weren't having any trouble when we left."

"Jah, they were holding their own with Gano," John agreed.

The men hung their straw hats on the pegs and headed into the kitchen for that cup of coffee that had been promised them. That's where the men were when Redbird and Beth entered the back door carrying a bucket half full of foamy goat milk between them.

Jim looked over into the bucket. "I sure am proud of you girls. I can't hardly believe my eyes."

"That is what I think," John agreed.

"How did you two get all that milk, and we couldn't?" Noah asked the girls.

Beth shrugged.

"Cause Gano likes us better than you," Redbird chirped.

"If that is so, milking the goat is your chore from now on," John said.

"We can do it," Redbird agreed.

*   *   *

An invitation had been announced at Sunday worship service about a quilting frolic to be held at Stella Strutt's house on Wednesday next.

Wednesday, so many women showed up that Mose had to set up two quilting frames in the living room.

Emma went. She planned to stop at Hal's later with all the news. Poor Hallie was missing out on so many frolics while she was laid up with that cast on her foot.

Margaret Yoder asked about Hal. She told Emma to express to Hal they missed her being with them that day. They hoped to see her and the new baby at the next quilting frolic. Emma relayed the message that they were welcome to stop at Hal's and meet the new Lapp baby.

Though the women knew from observation which members of the community were expecting a baby, it wasn't something they usually ever talked about. Each family only discussed an upcoming addition within the family. The quilters decided there might be a need for baby quilts to be given to families as gifts since new babies appeared routinely. That was the theme of this quilting frolic.

As soon as Mose put the frames together, the women unfolded the quilts that they pieced and tacked together with the filling and backing at the last frolic. In just a few minutes they had quilts rolled up on one side of the frames and stretched taut to the material covering the other end of the frames.

One set of frames had three crib quilts stretched on it for the boys. A trip around the world quilt in blue, green and pink blocks, and a flower garden in blue and white with yellow middles in the flowers. One was an Amish farmer boy blocks framed with blue strips. He wore black trousers, a yellow shirt and a straw hat.

On the other quilting frame were three crib quilts for girls. Two were the bow tie pattern. One set with pink bow ties, and the other with soft green. The third quilt was a Sunbonnet Sue, dressed in pink, in a large panel in the middle of the quilt. Nine patch blocks in pastel colors were around her for the border.

"Time to begin. Take your seats," Stella invited. "Take your seats."

The women, divided up three to each side of the frames. Jane Bontrager, Mary Mast, and Linda Yoder sat on one side of frame one with Wanda Bruner, Malinda Crumbhotz, and Metta Zook facing them. At the other frame was Margaret Yoder, Lovina Keim and Emma Keim facing Stella Strutt, Freda Stolfus, and Martha Briskey.

As they worked their needles through the quilt, the women chatted among themselves about common subjects: family, gardens, and others that might need various help from the community.

Quiet fell on the room when the women seemed to be all talked out. Jane Bontrager suggested they sing hymns until lunch time. In their chant like singing without music, they sang *In The Garden, Nearer My God To Thee*, and others.

As Stella Strutt glanced at the clock, she said, "Time to put lunch on the table. On the table, sure enough. Malinda, Metta and Mary, you come help me, help me. That leaves quilters to keep working on the quilts, working on the quilts."

Malinda Crumbhotz, Metta Zook and Mary Mast followed Stella Strutt into the kitchen to set up the potluck lunch furnished by the quilters.

In a few minutes, Emma was tired of sitting in one place. "Lovina and Martha, would you mind if I go to the kitchen to see if I can help? My legs are bothering me today. I feel the need to walk."

"Jah, that is fine with me," Martha Briskey said.

"Jah, we will keep working," Lovina assured her.

Emma was close to the door when she heard Stella mention Priscilla's name. She stopped to listen.

While Stella placed plates on the table, she reminded the other women, "Joseph Tefertiller's girl has always been a wild girl, a very wild girl. More likely than not the man that attacked her was someone she had been friendly with at one time or another. One time or another."

"Sister Stella, sure enough, you must not blame Joseph Tefertiller's Priscilla for what that evil man did," Mary Mast said softly. "No woman should be treated like that. I feel sorry for her. Bobby Keim has been keeping company with her, and they have become special friends."

Dressed in black like Stella, gray haired Metta Zook said, "I do not imagine Lovina Keim's Bobby will want to keep company with that woman now that she is second hand goods. He would do better if he looks elsewhere."

"Jah, I agree. Very much I agree," Stella chimed in.

"No one can fault Lovina Keim's Bobby if he changed his mind about Joseph Tefertiller's Priscilla. Sure enough," Malinda Crumbhotz, a short, stocky woman, agreed. "Though I do feel sorry for the poor girl. It will be hard for her to find a man now that word of what happened has gotten around."

"People should not fault Bobby Keim in this community. Not in this community," Stella agreed. "Joseph Tefertiller's Priscilla has reaped what she sowed. She reaped what she sewed. We all know that. Know that sure enough, ain't so?"

Emma's face flushed red as she marched into the kitchen with her hands balled into fists at her sides. "What Priscilla did during runspringa has nothing to do with what happened to her in Adam's shop. None of you should say these things about another person that is not here to defend herself. It might be one of us that evil man attacks next. Is there one among you that wants the rest of us to talk like this about you, if God forbid, it was you that was attacked?

We need to pray the sheriff catches the attacker soon before he harms another woman. In the meantime, you have no right to look down on Priscilla for something that was none of her doing. She has been a gute clerk in Adam's shop and a gute friend to me." Emma glared at Stella straight on. The woman puffed up for battle like a bloated, fat toad. "Nah, no one has the recht to look down on anyone else. Only God sits that high, and I can assure you he is on Priscilla's side, Stella Strutt."

She turned to escape to the quiet living room. Jane Bontrager was standing behind Emma, blocking the way. Emma could see the other quilters over Jane's shoulder. They had their heads down stitching. So intent at their sewing as if they didn't hear the conversation in the kitchen. They weren't fooling Emma. Not a sideways glance at each other with small talk. They were much too quiet. They heard all right.

Jane Bontrager winked at Emma as she stepped around her and entered the kitchen. Emma had to stay to see what Jane was going to do. Mary Mast came around the table to stand by Emma in the doorway. "I agree, Emma. If you hear of anything I can do for Priscilla Tefertiller please let me know. I want to help her and her family."

Jane agreed. "I feel the same way, Mary. Denki for your kindness. Those among us that are bothered by what happened to Priscilla should all pray for guidance in this matter."

"Praise the Lord, Jane. That is the kind of message I like to hear from this community. We need to stick together. Like I said next time it might be one of us that man attacks," Emma said pointedly, looking at Stella Strutt. "We would want people to be concerned about us."

"Voonderball gute message to end this subject on," Jane said. "Now lets enjoy our fellowship lunch and go back to quilting. We should get all six done before we leave this afternoon, ain't so? I'm starving. Sister Stella, are you ready for the rest of us to come to the table?"

"Jah," Stella said sharply. "Jah indeed."

"Gute," Jane stepped to the door. "Sisters, we are ready to eat lunch now." As soon as they gathered in the kitchen, Jane said, "Before we eat we all have silent prayers to say to ask for God's understanding. Bow your heads, Sisters."

Chapter 9

The conversation at the table and for most of the afternoon was strained. By three in the afternoon, they finished quilting and took the quilts off the frames. Six of the women said they would take one of the quilts home and hem around the edges.

Before they left, Mary Mast suggested they sit down in their chairs and finish the quilting frolic with a prayer.

Margaret Yoder suggested that Jane Bontrager start the prayer and each of them would add to it.

Jane Bontrager said that was a good idea.

"Nah, I do not think that is gute. Not gute at all," Stella Strutt protested "Jane can give the whole prayer. The whole prayer indeed."

"I for one think it is a gute idea," Margaret Yoder said, ignoring the glare Stella gave her. "You start now, Jane."

"Let us bow our heads. God, we say denki to You for allowing us to have this voonderball gute day of fellowship at our quilting frolic. Keep us thinking about compassion for others." Jane stopped.

Mary Mast took over. "God, my thoughts and prayers are for a special person here with us. I know the pain I felt when You took my first born home to heaven. I would please ask that you give others in our community time to enjoy their newborns. Help us come together to so others the recht path to travel."

Several of the women said softly, "Praise the Lord."

"God, it is Your word I want to remind us *all* of," Linda Yoder prayed. "Your word says if we hold anything against anyone, forgive him, so that You our father in heaven may forgive us our sins. I believe that to be true and those among us that do not follow that word should take heed."

"Amen to that," the other women muttered.

"Denki for all our family, friends and people in this community that come together to help each other," Wanda Bruner prayed.

"Denki for this gute day and for all the work we were able to do to get so many quilts done at once. We send all the praise in your name," Malinda Crumbhotz prayed.

Metta Zook said, "God, denki for all the children in our house that have gotten over chicken pox and now are healthy again."

"That brought titters from some of the women who knew what it was like to nurse ailing children.

Metta turned in her seat to look behind her at the other frame. "Margaret, you are next."

Margaret prayed, "God, You have said be kind and compassionate to one another, forgiving each other, just as in Christ God forgave you. Let us remember that."

"God, it sometimes is a failing of humans to forget compassion and kindness. We need to lean on You God to help us remember to treat others this way," Lovina Keim prayed.

Emma was next. She had the feeling Stella Strutt was the target of the prayers. She was already in enough trouble with Stella so she was not going to heap more on Stella than she already had. She prayed, "God, denki for my two precious babies. I ask you for a miracle for my baby boy if it is your will."

Everyone waited for the next prayer. After a few seconds, Emma opened her eyes. "Stella, it is your ..... . She is not here! Where did she go."

The others opened their eyes and stared at Stella's empty chair.

Jane called, "Stella, where are you?"

"I am coming. Jah, I am coming." Stella came from the

kitchen with a large tray of glasses and a pitcher of lemonade. "Before you go home, I thought you might like a cool drink. A cool drink sure enough."

When Emma visited Hallie later that afternoon to fill her in about the quilting bee, she told her step-mother what the women said about Priscilla. Emma admitted she now felt remorse for the way she scolded the four women in the kitchen. It wasn't her place to do that. If only Stella Strutt hadn't instigated the condemnation of Priscilla in her presence.

Hal tried not to smile. She was proud of the way Emma stood up for her friend. "That's my Emma. You let them have it. That's what I would have done."

Emma smiled weakly. "I am not you. Sure enough, it did help that I was not alone in the way I think. Jane and Mary Mast backed me. Even most of the other women added comments in the prayer to show Stella they did not agree with her."

"That just goes to show you there are others in the community that aren't as narrow minded as Stella Strutt. Gute for you and the others for standing up to Stella," Hal declared, clapping her hands.

"I wish you would not take this so lightly. Sure enough, it was funny how Stella left the room before her turn to add to the prayer. We were surprised to find her seat empty."

Hal looked mystified. "Really? I can't imagine her being able to tiptoe quietly from a room as heavy as she is."

"Jah, she did it and came back carrying lemonade for all of us after we opened our eyes and found her missing. That was a gute drink, but none of us were fooled. It was her way to keep from having to partake in the prayer, because some of us did not think like her.

Hallie, Stella Strutt is not the sort of person who likes to be brow beaten in front of her guests. In her own home no less. I am afraid Stella blames me for what happened during the prayer. She will get even with me somehow," Emma declared.

"Ach! Don't worry about Stella. Knowing her, she will put her attention on someone else before long. You know she picks on everyone in the community at one time or another. It's just

Stella's way like it or not," Hal said.

"I agree. I have seen how she torments you, and I would just as soon miss my turn in Stella Strutt's hot seat. Denki very much," Emma protested.

That sent Hal into a fit of laughter. Emma couldn't hold her sour face. She had to laugh, too.

The month of May ended with a Saturday birthday party for Redbird and Beth. The girls loved being the center of attention and getting gifts didn't hurt. They loved their cakes made by Mammi and Aunt Tootie and the homemade ice cream was a special treat.

The month of June was uneventful. Emma stayed home and tried to rest like Hal wanted her to do. Being alone during the day made her jumpy. She'd hear a noise outside and ease to each window to look out, fearing she'd see the red sports car sitting in the driveway. She didn't bother to tell anyone how nervous she was. Hal would probably insist she stay at their house so she could rest better. Adam might agree with Hal. Emma didn't want that. She wasn't about to let some crazy Englisher chase her from her home.

At the next Sunday worship service, Emma was pretty sure Jane Bontrager told Elton what was said at Stella Strutt's quilting frolic. The sermons from the three preachers were aimed at Stella and her narrow mindedness. All of which just made Emma certain if she went to another quilting frolic at Stella Strutt's house, Stella would crucify her by tacking her to the quilting frame.

After the first hymn, Deacon Enos Yutzy came forward to read bible scripture. The deacon started with Proverbs, "He coveteth greedily all the day long: but the righteous giveth and spareth not.

From the book of James, he read, "Therefore, my beloved brethren, let every man be swift to hear, slow to speak, slow to wrath."

He thumbed the bible to a bookmark in Colossians. "Forebearing one another, and forgiving one another, if any against any: even as Christ forgave you also do ye." Deacon Yutzy closed his bible as he looked around the congregation.

Then he nodded at Luke Yoder before he sat.

Luke stood up and looked around the room. "I want to focus on an animal. One that you usually would not bid on at the salebarn during a horse sale. You have all thought many times this animal was not worth the feed and shelter to bring home.

There he would be, standing alone in the ring. Who knows how long he'd been waiting in the back with a pen to himself. No one wanted their animals put in with him. I am talking about a lowly donkey. The most insignificant of animals with an inconsequential life. No thoroughbred blood running through his veins. His next meal was his only solace, because he was of no use to anyone. He was a laborer with no denki said to him. A meaningless creature according to every farmer. Anyway, that is how the donkey felt, because no one wanted anything to do with him.

Have any of you in this community had something happen to you that questioned your significance? Have you felt like giving up on family or your daily life? Ach! The next time you ponder your purpose in life, think about how that donkey felt." Luke stopped talking and rubbed his blond beard. "Did any of you ever stop to think that Jesus asked for such a donkey as the one at the salebarn? Jesus could have asked for any method of transportation, but He chose a donkey to ride. Uniquely qualified, this nobody donkey's purpose was to carry Jesus, and the animal was gute at his job.

So we should all keep in mind. There are those among us that need our help to feel better about themselves. We should seek them out and do what God wants us to do. Choose them to help like Jesus chose the lowly donkey."

After a kneel down prayer by everyone, Preacher Yoder nodded at Bishop Bontrager and sat.

Emma didn't think she had ever seen Elton's face as red as it was that morning. He waddled forward and straighten his body to its full height. He held his bible against his chest. "I have a parable to tell you this morning. If there was ever a time to tell you this parable, it is now so I am going to talk about a donkey, too. Perhaps, this was the same lowly donkey as the one Preacher Yoder told us about.

One day a farmer's donkey fell into a dry well. The animal cried piteously for hours as the farmer tried to figure out what to do.

Finally, he decided the animal was old, and was not worth much since he was just a donkey. Besides, the dry well needed to be filled up already. It just wasn't worth it to the farmer to get the donkey out of the well. He invited his neighbor men to come over and help him fill in the well. Their wives could fix a lunch for the men, and the children could play games.

The farmer had asked his neighbors to bring their own shovels as he did not have enough shovels for everybody. They heard the donkey's cries from far away at the bottom of the well, but the farmer said it was all recht to bury the animal in the well. So the farmers circled around the well and began to shovel dirt into the opening.

At first, the donkey realized what was happening and cried with fright. Suddenly to everyone's amazement, he quieted down. A few more shovel loads spilled in the well. The farmers grew curious to know if they had covered up the donkey. They peeked down into the hole, and was very surprised at what they saw. As each shovel full of dirt fell on the donkey, he had shook it off his back. He did something that amazed the farmers. After he had shaken off the shovels of dirt, he took a step up. As the farmer's neighbors continued to shovel dirt on top of the animal, he'd shake it off and take another step up. To the farmer's chagrin, the other farmers continued to throw in dirt just so they could watch the donkey climb higher and higher.

Finally, the farmers cheered for the donkey as the animal stepped up over the edge of the well and trotted off.

The donkey's owner, now impressed as much as his neighbors by the donkey's effort to live, yelled after him, "Go with God and be free. You deserved it."

The moral of this parable should be clear to all of you. Life shovels dirt on all of us, all kinds of dirt. The trick to not giving in to that dirt is to take one step up at a time. Each of our troubles is a stepping stone. We can get out of the deepest wells just by not stopping to be buried by the trouble. We need to accept what happens to us, God's sheep, as God's Will and never give up. How does this work best? It helps if you feel God's love and the love of your family and friends cheering you on like the farmers did the donkey.

So for those of you in our community that do not feel a shovel of dirt hitting you right now, but know someone who does, go to them and offer your support. I am sure all of us know of someone around us at this very minute that could use our help.

Now, John Lapp, it is time for a hymn. You will lead."

Two hymns and the final prayer later it was time for the announcements by Bishop Bontrager.

John Lapp relaid to Elton the message from the sheriff department for him to pass on. Bishop Bontrager announced a total of six attacks on women had been made in Wickenburg. In all instances, a pillow case was on the victim's head so the sheriff department knew it was the same man.

Sheriff Dawson said he wanted the word passed around that this was a serial rapist. People were to be careful when they walked on the road by going in groups. He suggested young girls should not be allowed to walk alone or go to the mailbox until this man is caught.

No more swimming in Bender Creek by the young ones until further notice. If a suspicious Englisher drives by an Amish house several times a day let the sheriff know what the car looks like.

Lock doors at night and pass on any suspicions to the sheriff department. Sheriff Dawson said he needed all the help he can get from our community to catch this man before he hurts another woman or kills one. This man is dangerous so do not try to catch him yourselves. In the meantime, the sheriff will send patrol cars out on the country roads at all times of day and night for our protection so we are not to be concerned when we see them drive by.

*   *   *

After supper that evening, everyone sat out on the porch,

watching the lightning bugs. Hal felt well enough to have John and Jim help her hop outside to sit in the porch swing. They placed the cradle close to her so she could keep an eye on the baby.

Hal invited Emma and Nora to sit with her. Aunt Tootie pulled a chair over by the swing. The men sat in chairs on the other end while Noah and Daniel dangled their legs over the edge of the porch.

Hal said to Emma, "Have you heard any news about Priscilla?"

"Jah, I asked Polly about her at the fellowship lunch. There has been no change. She said Priscilla is hiding in her room. She doesn't come out for the family. Polly is the only one she lets in her room, and that is to bring her food and clean clothes. She will not discuss what happened with her mother. I just cannot sit still and do nothing to help her. I am going to go see Priscilla whether she likes it or not. It might help, Hallie, if you have a talk to Priscilla too."

Hal shook her head no. "I don't think I should do that unless Priscilla asks for me as a nurse."

"It's a pity the man who attacked that poor girl hasn't been found yet," Nora said.

"Down right scary if you ask me," Tootie agreed.

Jim nodded. "You know he has to be lurking around, waiting to attack another girl."

"I am sure of it," Emma said. "You heard at the worship service what the sheriff said. There had been six such attacks in Wickenburg so far in the last few months."

"When the sheriff told you this news, did he say if any of the women could describe the man at all?" John asked.

Emma shook her head up and down. "The sheriff thinks the women were all attacked by the same man. He sneaks up behind them and pulls a pillow case over their heads so they cannot see him. They struggled, and he beat them senseless. They had no idea who the man was except that he smells like strong English cologne."

John said, "The bishop was recht to tell everyone we must keep our eyes open for a stranger hanging around our community. Someone that we feel we cannot trust."

Daniel elbowed Noah. With a nod of his head, he said, "We should tell them what we saw." They twisted around on the end of the porch.

Noah said, "Daniel just reminded me of something. We have seen a shiny red car driving slowly by the swimming hole at Bender Creek several times. The driver seemed to be paying close attention to us."

Daniel added, "We were all walking home last Saturday afternoon when the man stopped Katie Bender and asked for directions to Keim's Furniture Shop. She told him how to get there, thinking he wanted to buy furniture. He asked Katie if she'd like to take a ride in his new car and show him where the shop was. He claimed to not be too good with directions and not familiar with the country roads. She told him she did not ride with strangers and walked back to the rest of us."

Noah added, "That was one time. In a couple days after that, the same man was back again and stopped another girl, Beth Zook. She refused to ride with him when he asked her. He saw a bunch of us boys coming at him and took off in a hurry."

"You heard the bishop say you cannot go to Bender Creek until we know it is safe. You must abide by that," Jim reminded them.

John agreed. "Sounds like the recht place a man would target young girls. One of them is likely to take a ride with him. We need to call Sheriff Dawson. He should know about this."

"I have seen that man the boys saw and more than once," Emma said. That cause Adam to take notice. "He stopped me back in April by the mailbox here. He asked me if I wanted to ride in his new car. I walked away from him."

"You didn't tell me that, and you didn't think that was odd?" Hal asked.

"I did mention the man to you sort of. That was the man who asked me if the vegetable stand was open yet. I did not think much about it except the man made me uneasy by the way he kept pestering me to get me to talk to him, and the creepy way he looked at me. He drove his car close by me until

I turned into the driveway then he raced off.

The problem is that is not the first time I noticed him. Last fall, he was at our fund raiser at Luke Yoder's farm. He made a point of talking to me while I gave the girls a pony ride. Again he showed up at the school's open house and talked to me in the lunch line. Actually, he was a real pest that time," Emma said. "Sure enough, if the sheriff needs a description of him I can give a gute one and what his car looks like. Adam, we will go by the phone shed before we go home so I can call Sheriff Dawson. I want him to know this might be the very man he should be looking for."

Chapter 10

Monday morning, Emma decided she was driving to the Tefertiller farm and insist Priscilla see her. The farm was four miles from the Keim farm. It didn't take long to get to her destination. Any other time, the drive would have been a pleasant one for Emma as she watched for pheasants, turkeys and quail in the pastures. Not this morning. Worrying about what Priscilla would do when she knew she had company, she was on edge when she pulled into the Tefertiller driveway.

She walked up the porch steps of the large, two story house, white and austere clean similar to all Amish farm houses. Emma looked behind her toward the outbuildings, a large barn and a chicken house. She heard soft grunts from a sow with piglets in one of the A huts for farrowing sows in the grassy pen. The doors to the feed shed and tool shed were closed.

Joseph and Polly Tefertiller had six children. Three of them, older than Priscilla, were gone from home. The two younger ones, boys, were old enough to help their father. No one came to meet her so Emma knocked on the door.

Polly Tefertiller was a lanky, dark brown haired woman in her late forties. Emma saw an older version of Priscilla when Polly opened the door. "Wilcom. Gute to see you, Emma. Come in. Coffee pot is hot yet."

"Denki, but I have given up coffee for hot tea," Emma said as she followed Polly to the kitchen.

"Sit down and visit with me while I fix your tea. It does not take long, and I could use a cup myself," Polly invited. "I suspect you have a reason for coming today. I must tell you I am very worried about my daughter's health."

"That is why I am here. I also worry about Priscilla. From what you have told me at Sunday worship service, Priscilla has been slow to bounce back. I had thought maybe if I gave her time she would work things out. So has there been any change at all?"

"Nah, she is the same," Polly said wearily as she set a cup of tea in front of Emma and one where she intended to sit.

Emma said, "That is too bad. I wanted to give her time to mend before I came, but now I think too much time to herself is not gute," Emma said.

Polly wrapped her hands around her warm cup. "My daughter is physically much better, but she is not so mentally. She needs someone to talk to about what happened. She will not do it with me. Maybe you are the answer to my prayers for Priscilla."

"I do not know about that, but I want to help her. Could I see her now?" Emma asked.

"Jah," Polly said, "but she might not let you in to visit. She stays holed up in her room and does not talk much to me when I bring her meals. Just stays in her bed, staring at the wall."

"I will not stay long if it upsets Priscilla. I feel she cannot get over what happened to her by hiding from everyone. She has to start facing us." Emma tipped her cup up for the last sip, got up and headed for the stairs.

She tapped on Priscilla's bedroom door. "It is Emma." When no answer came, she announced louder, "Priscilla, can I come in?"

"I wish you did not want to see me. Go away." Priscilla's voice sounded muffled.

Emma opened the door and stepped inside the room. Priscilla, covered up to the neckline of her white, cotton nightgown, avoiding eye contact with Emma just as her mother said. She raised the covers even higher until her face was covered.

The room was so dismal, dimly lit with only what light came through the top half of the bedroom window. Emma felt that was enough to depress anyone.

She crossed her arms over her chest. "I am not going away. I am worried about you, and so is everyone else." She sat down in the wooden chair by the bed. Priscilla peeled the covers back, and tears formed in her eyes. She slowly turned her head to look at her friend. Emma reached out and squeezed her limp hand. Priscilla jerked away and put her hand under the cover. "Believe me, you cannot stay in hiding forever. You have to face your family and friends. It is time to come back to the living."

Priscilla sucked in a shuddering breath as she eyed Emma. Her bruised, swollen face made Emma hurt when she looked at Priscilla. Knowing the reason why the young woman looked that way made it difficult for Emma to concentrate on why she came. The queasy feeling rising in the pit of her stomach made her want to leave as Priscilla had told her to do.

If only she could put Priscilla and her problems out of her mind. Instantly, it came to her she needed to pray to stay strong and be compassionate for Priscilla's sake. Those signs of a hard fought battle were going to stay on Priscilla's face for some time. Emma had to get used to seeing the bruises and cuts.

Bolstering all the strength she had, Emma looked directly at Priscilla. "Bobby Keim is beside himself with worry. When can he come see you?"

"Never! I cannot face him. Not now. Not ever. My life with him is ruined. He needs to forget me." The tears flooded down her face telling Emma what Priscilla said wasn't the way she wanted it to be. Priscilla stared at the ceiling as she brushed away the wetness on her cheeks with the back of her hand.

"Sheriff Dawson asked me to talk to you, but he is anxious to talk to you himself about what happened. Any little clue could be enough to find this man. You are not the only one he has hurt. There has been at least six other women around Wickenburg he has attacked," Emma told her.

"Nah, I cannot talk to the sheriff, because I cannot face him or anyone else. There is nothing I can tell him. I just want to forget this awful nightmare that happened to me, but as hard as I try I cannot," Priscilla said dolefully.

Emma tried a quiet tone. "The sheriff said he knew you might feel that way. He asked me to talk to you for him so that he could leave you alone a while longer. Tell me who attacked you."

Red blotches mottled Priscilla's pale face. "Like I said I have nothing to tell the sheriff or you. I did not see the man. He came up behind me and put something over my head."

"Jah, he did. It was a pillow case. Can you remember about the way he spoke? Maybe with an accent?" Emma questioned

"I want to block that ugly time out of my mind. I do not want to keep remembering details," Priscilla said shrilly. "Please do not ask me to think about this. All I can think about now is why did God let this awful thing happen to me?"

"What you are going through is hard for you, but do not blame God. It is the fault of the man that harmed you. I cannot understand why anyone would do this awful deed to you or any woman. I do know the man does not know God to be able to do something so terrible to another human being," Emma assured her. "So did you have anyone come in the shop that afternoon?"

Priscilla looked toward the window until she could keep her voice steady and quiet. She twisted her head to look at Emma. "Jah, right after lunch Albert Jostle came. He asked for a job. I had my back to the door when the bell jingled. Anyone would know when Albert was in the room without seeing him first. I never seen such a schooslich (poky, clumsy) person. He walks across a floor with big clunky steps and his elbows out like a cocky rooster. I think his shoes are two sizes too large for him. That makes them heavy on his feet."

"Was Albert there long?" Emma asked.

Priscilla shook her head. "Nah, I told him he would have to come back to talk to Adam later before we closed, because Adam did the hiring. He left right away."

"Are you sure he left?" Emma quizzed.

"Jah, I could see out the window when he walked on the

road toward home. He said he would be back later," Priscilla said dully.

Emma pushed, "So he is the only one you remember?"

Priscilla's head bobbed up and down. "Jah."

"What were you doing when you were attacked?" Emma asked.

Priscilla thought a second. "I was dusting the birdhouses."

"So you had your back to the door when the bell sounded again," Emma stated.

"Jah." Priscilla looked puzzled. "Only I did not hear the bell that time."

"Can it be silenced?"

"I do not know," Priscilla groaned.

"I will ask Adam about that. How did you come to know you were not alone?"

Priscilla's face turned ashen as she relived the event. "A hand came in front of my face and held my mouth shut. A man's voice said for me to keep still. He just wanted to be friendly, but I remember thinking I did not think his voice sounded friendly. It was an Englisher speaking. I am sure of that. Next thing I knew he threw a piece of material over my eyes and tied it behind. He turned loose of me and jumped over the counter beside me. I fought him as he pushed me to the floor."

Emma fisted her hands in her lap at the thought of what happened next. "You certainly did. All we have to do is look at you to see how brave you were. Did he say anything else to you?"

Priscilla thought for a moment and nodded. "Jah, he did say something odd."

Emma hoped for a clue. "What was it?"

"You aren't the one I expected to be here." Priscilla looked puzzled then she shrugged. "No matter. After he said that, he tore at my clothes. I struggled as hard as I could. I really did, Emma. The man hit me in the face with his fist again and again. I felt myself slipping into darkness. I am glad I do not remember anything else.

That is probably the only gute thing about this whole mess.

Every waking moment, I can imagine what I was put through. At night, the nightmares haunt me so I cannot sleep. That is bad enough." Priscilla sobbed as she put her hands over her ears to shut out any more questions. She doubled up in a ball, trying to stop the awful scenes from entering her mind. "Please do not make me talk about what happened."

"You need to talk about it," Emma said loudly to make sure she heard.

"I do not want to," Priscilla retorted.

"That seems to be true, but it is gute for you to do so. Perhaps, this man had been a customer. Did you think the man's voice sounded familiar?"

"Nah, I had never heard it before," Priscilla affirmed.

"It did not sound like Albert?" Emma probed.

"Nah, I am sure of that. Why?"

"You said he was coming back to talk to Adam. I know he came back. I saw him come out of the shop and head for home before I came in and found you," Emma answered

"I did not see him again, but it was not his voice I heard when I was attacked," Priscilla insisted.

"I told the sheriff I saw Albert leave the shop in a hurry just before I found you. He must have seen you on the floor and ran off scared. The sheriff was going to talk to him. Just one more question. Did you smell anything like scents coming from this man?"

Priscilla thought a moment. "Jah, he smelled of cigarette smoke and an English strong after shave."

Just what Emma thought Priscilla might answer. Sounded like she was talking about the man in the red sports car. "That is a gute start. I will tell the sheriff. He may not bother you, but I cannot promise that he will not. He has to find the person who attacked you, and recht now that is a priority for his department. It is his job to question you. Sure enough, he would be better at asking the recht questions. Once you feel like getting out of this room, you tell your daed to call the sheriff to tell him you will talk to him. Another thing, you need to let Bobby know when he can come see you."

"Nah, I told you Bobby cannot come. I meant that. I do not

think I will ever feel gute enough to face Bobby. I do not want to see the look on his face. Sure enough, I do not want to hear how awful he thinks I am now that I am second hand goods. Anything he has to say would only make me hurt more," Priscilla rolled over and turn her back to Emma again. "Now go away!"

Emma persisted though she knew she was losing the argument. "Bobby is not thinking anything of the sort. He just wants to see you, because he is so worried about you. He will tell you he loves you and misses you if you would just give him a chance." It was then Emma thought of another tact. "You should be checked again soon. Can Nurse Hal come?"

"Nah, I do not want to see Nurse Hal. There is nothing she can do for me. It would be a waste of her time. Now go away." Priscilla covered her head up.

Emma gave up. She walked downstairs and stopped in the kitchen to tell Priscilla's mother she was leaving. "Polly, denki for letting me see Priscilla. She feels bad about what happened to her as any woman would. That is natural. Since she has faced me once, I think she will talk to me again. I will come back."

Polly sighed in relief. "Jah, that is a hopeful start."

"Jah, and I told her Sheriff Dawson may drop by. He had me ask Priscilla some questions, but he will have to follow up. She will have to see him some time or other."

"I will make sure he does talk to Priscilla. The man who attacked my daughter needs to be caught." Polly's voice sounded as dismal as her daughter felt.

"Would you mind if Nurse Hal checked on Priscilla soon? I asked Priscilla, and she said no. I feel Nurse Hal knows what to say to get Priscilla to snap out of this so I want her to visit," Emma said.

"Sure enough, it would be a gute idea. My daughter is in terrible shape. It looks like she is going to hold up in her room the rest of her life," Polly worried. "Though I do not expect Nurse Hal will be able to come soon."

"Sure enough, Hallie is not able to visit recht away. She is regaining her strength, and baby Johnnie is growing stronger every day. It is the cast on her foot that makes walking cumbersome until she gets used to it. When she gets her strength back from childbirth, she will get out more. Maybe by the time Hallie can travel, Priscilla will change her mind." It passed through Emma's mind she'd have to work on Hallie, too. Nurse Hal meant it when she said the only way she'd come to the Tefertiller farm was if Priscilla consented to see her.

"Praise the Lord, you are such a gute friend to my Priscilla. I know my daughter was not friendly today. She hasn't been nice to me when I take her meals. Come as often as you can. Sure enough, that is gute news about Nurse Hal. I pray for her, the baby and Priscilla every day," Polly said.

Emma gave her a hug. "Denki for your prayers for Hallie and the baby. So will I pray for Priscilla. Try not to wear yourself out with worry. I am going to see Priscilla through this."

On her way home, Emma stopped to see how Hal was doing. After Hal scolded her for not staying home to rest, Emma told her the reason she felt she had to leave home. She had been to check on Priscilla. Just as soon as she finished her visit with Hal she would be on her way home.

"My instructions still go. You stay home. Taking care of yourself first is a must recht now," Hal ordered.

Emma crossed her arms over her chest and cupped her elbows in her hands. "I just stopped by to tell you how I found Priscilla. You want to hear about her before I leave or not."

"I'm sorry, Emma. Go ahead and tell me your news," Hal relented.

Emma explained how Priscilla treated her and what she said.

"Sounds like normal emotions coming out given the circumstances. As bad as I hate to say this, the best thing you can do for Priscilla is continue to go see her now that she's willing to talk to you. That's a gute sign," Hal encouraged.

"Priscilla is not all that willing. At first, she did not let me in. She told me to go away. I barged in anyway and told her I came to talk to her. I was staying until I did," Emma declared.

"That's my Emma." Hal grinned at her then she lost the

grin to give Emma advice. "You cannot do all the talking. You have to listen so Priscilla gets all the emotions out in the open. She has to work her way through the trauma. She needs a friend to listen that she feels won't condemn her."

"I wish you could go see her to assess the way she is," Emma said.

"I can when she's ready to see me. I want her to give me permission to visit with her first. It's gute enough for recht now that she lets you come. When I'm able to climb in the buggy to go to Gemeesunndaag (worship services) and sit in a chair to eat my meals, I'll feel better about getting out. Recht now, I have to think about the baby. He needs tender, loving care until he grows strong, and I'm dragging around this dead weight the doctor calls a cast which is a bother," Hal reminded her.

Emma's clamped her lips shut to keep from smiling. "Awk, gute. I know my baby brother has to come first. Mammi or Aunt Tootie can stay with him so he does not have to leave home if he is not ready. I will be glad to go with you to see Priscilla when the time comes."

Before she fixed supper Emma knew she should call Sheriff Dawson. She wanted to tell him what she found out from Priscilla. Maybe it would be enough information, if she asked the right questions, to keep the sheriff from bothering Priscilla. She drove by her driveway to the phone shed and rifled through the Wickenburg phone book until she found the sheriff office number.

A woman answered on the second ring.

Emma asked to speak to the sheriff. The woman said just a minute and put her on hold. When the sheriff picked up the phone, Emma told him in detail about Priscilla's memories of the assault. "Sheriff, Priscilla smelled cigarette smoke and after shave cologne just like I did on the man in the red car."

"We're trying our best to run down that car and man by the description you gave me, Mrs. Keim," Sheriff Dawson said.

"Priscilla was sure the man who assaulted her was not Albert," Emma told him.

"I talked to the boy, and I didn't feel like he was guilty," the sheriff shared. "I did lecture him on the need to report a crime like this. That woman was badly hurt and needed medical attention. He shouldn't have ran off like that and kept still."

"Sure enough, Albert is young yet. He does not see much, living on that farm. Lots of people get ohnmechtich (fainty) when they see a person's blood. You have to admit there was plenty of blood around Priscilla. Her head in a pillow case might have spooked Albert, ain't so? He probably thought she was dead, and he did not want to touch her," Emma excused, feeling sorry for this second time she put Albert in Sheriff Dawson's focus.

"I reckon that is so," Dawson agreed.

"One other thing. Priscilla said the only words the man spoke to her was you aren't the one I expected to be here. She was sure he sounded English," Emma said.

The other end of the line went silent.

"Sheriff Dawson, you still there?" She asked.

"Yes, I was just thinking. Didn't you tell me you have seen this man you told me about several times?"

"Jah, I did. He seems to always make a point of talking to me until I make it clear I do not want to be near him," Emma said.

"Knowing that, what do you think the man who attacked Priscilla Tefertiller meant when he told her she wasn't the one he expected to be in your husband's furniture shop?" The sheriff quizzed.

Emma broke out in a weak sweat as she processed what the sheriff was hinting. "You think he expected to find me working in the shop since it belongs to Adam?"

"I sure do. I want you to keep your doors locked and windows shut and locked. Maybe get a baseball bat from your brothers to use for protection. Take all the precautions you can to be safe until we catch this man. I'm going to send a squad car by your house routinely. You can't be too careful. Do you understand me?"

"Jah, I understand," Emma said.

"Thanks for getting the information from Priscilla. Any idea yet when I can interview her myself?"

Emma replied, "I told her you want to speak with her so she is aware of it. What I did was just go to the Tefertiller house and confront her. Her face shows she was through a battle, but I think she is very depressed. You can do the same thing I did and just show up. Priscilla is expecting you so she will most likely see you."

"All right, keep me posted if anything comes up," the sheriff said. "You hide if that man comes to your house in a red car. He is too dangerous to try to confront. Get one of your brothers' baseball bats to fend him off if he breaks in."

"Denki, Sheriff, I understand. I will hide," Emma agreed.

That evening as bad as she hated to mention her conversation with the sheriff, Emma told Adam first about her visit with Priscilla. After that, she told him she called the sheriff. She relayed the dire conversation about the attacker possibly wanting to find her at the shop instead of Priscilla.

Adam frowned when he realized how much danger his wife was in.

"The sheriff said he was sending a squad car by here often to make sure the red car wasn't in the area. He wanted me to lock the house doors. I did not tell him we do not have locks on the doors. What he does not know will not hurt him or get me another lecture on safety," Emma scoffed.

Adam wrote, "Ach! This is serious. I am putting locks on the doors after supper. The sheriff is recht about making this house safe for you. What else did he say?"

"I should keep all the windows closed and locked, and ask my brothers for a baseball bat to use on an intruder," Emma said grinning as she thought of herself wielding a baseball bat for protection.

"Does your mother still have some of those tear gas canisters she bought when the Hostellers were breaking in on people?" Adam wrote.

"I do not know, but I can ask," Emma said, rubbing her tight stomach. The twins must have rolled into a ball, hugging each other. At least, that was what she wanted to think was happening.

So for the rest of June, Emma's only outings were to

worship service and to visit Priscilla with a brief stop to tell Hallie how the visits went and to hold her baby brother.

Then it was the end of June. She still had two months to go to delivery date, but she knew Doctor Burns was just waiting at one of her next checkups to spring a C-section date on her and Adam. She'd like to be glad about greeting her babies into the world, but she dreaded what was happening to one of her twins. His prospects of living were slim if Doctor Burns was right. She had to live with that knowledge and try with God's help to come to terms with it. Except just yet she didn't know how she was going to do it.

Chapter 11

Three hot and humid summer weeks passed. Being pregnant in unbearable heat made Emma miserable. She spent her free time under a shade tree in back of the house. Safely, out of sight from the road so if by chance the red car came by, the man wouldn't see her. Emma pulled a white hanky out of her apron pocket. She wiped away the sweat beads under her eyes and continued fanning with a paper fan handed out by the feed store in Wickenburg.

By the end of July, Emma had been checking on Priscilla twice a week. Driving back and forth at least gave her a little breeze and a break from sitting in one place suffering from the heat. Twice she had a sheriff patrol car pass her on the road and the deputy waved at her. To Emma, the deputy was just a reminder of how much danger she and every other woman was in at the moment.

At first, she didn't see much improvement in her friend. When Emma finely felt encouraged was the day Priscilla wanted to know what kind of day it was outside. She asked what type of jobs, Adam was doing at the moment. Emma felt that was a turning point for Priscilla when she seemed interested in things outside her room again. Maybe she was ready to get out of her room.

One morning, Emma ventured with, "Nurse Hal would like to come check on you. As a nurse that is. Will you let her?"

"Nah." Priscilla snapped. She paused, running a finger

around the blocks on her nine patch quilt while she thought. "Jah, I think I want her to come."

"Voonderball gute!" Emma calmed herself at the seething look Priscilla gave her. "Sure enough, I will let her know."

Emma didn't see why Hal couldn't go visit Priscilla. Baby John was doing fine. The family called him Johnnie now. Everyone agreed that name seemed more fitting for a baby. He'd be fine in Mammi Nora's care while Hal was away from home.

Hal took the baby to worship services now so Emma had high hopes that her stepmother would feel up to visiting Priscilla soon. She stopped by the Lapp farm. Hal agreed to go the next morning while Nora and Tootie watched the baby. He'd sleep most of the morning so she just had to be home in time to let him nurse when he woke up.

The next day, Emma pulled in at the Lapp farm and parked behind Dawdi Jim's car. Hal limped out to greet her so Emma didn't have to climb down. "You can help me in and out of your buggy. I have a little trouble climbing since this cast weighs me down." Emma leaned over and took hold of Hal's hand to help her.

Once Emma had her settled on the seat, Hal said, "When we get there, I want to see Priscilla alone. Maybe she will be more willing to open up. You could be a help to Polly by talking to her while I'm with Priscilla. If Priscilla is still willing, you can talk to her after I've finished my visit."

"I have seen her so many times. It will not bother me if she does not want to visit with me. Ach!" Emma burst out with.

"Was ist letz?" Hal asked.

"I just remembered that Priscilla's room is upstairs. I need to see her long enough to talk her into coming downstairs to the living room for your visit. You should not try walking up those steps," Emma declared.

"Stairs is one thing I haven't tackled with this cast yet so Priscilla meeting me downstairs would be gute. If she wants to see me bad enough, it's a gute way to get her out of that room," Hal said

"It is gute you are going to visit with her. I am so afraid I will say the wrong thing. I did not want to act too sympathetic and help her stay in self pity," Emma worried.

Hal said, "Priscilla needs time to heal. The worse thing you can do is tell her she is wallowing in self pity. She feels as if she doesn't have a life left that is worth anything. She values what other people think of her. Recht now she thinks she sure enough is second hand goods. Listen to her. That's gute, and make sure she knows you're there for her when she needs you."

Emma rubbed a thumb over the lines as she spoke, "The last time I was there, I asked again if Bobby could come see her. She still said nah."

"I know Bobby must be worried sick and missing Priscilla so much. Maybe he should just go to her like you do, uninvited," Hal suggested.

"It worked for the sheriff to come out uninvited, but I told Priscilla she had to talk to him. He would not give her a choice," Emma said.

"On second thought," Hal paused.

"Go on," Emma said.

"You should ask Bobby to come see me before he does a surprise visit. He'll be more apt to say the wrong things than you are."

"I will talk to Bobby soon," Emma said.

"You are so gute to do this for Bobby and Priscilla, but you need your rest. Try not to worry so much about Priscilla. This will work itself out. God will see to it," Hal said.

"Jah, I know. Whatever happens is God's will," Emma stated in a rote tone.

"In your case, I think God would prefer you helped yourself some," Hal said.

As soon as Emma had Hal settled on the living room couch, she explained to Polly that Hal couldn't climb the stairs. She'd bring Priscilla downstairs.

Polly said she had sent the other children off on errands so they wouldn't be in the way. She hoped Emma had good luck talking Priscilla out of her room.

In a few minutes, Emma came downstairs with Priscilla following her. Emma winked at Hal. "I am going to the kitchen and talk to Polly. Call me if you need anything."

Hal slid over on the couch and patted the seat. "Come sit by me. It is so gute to see you dressed. I'm glad you wanted to come downstairs since I'm limited as to where I can go." She pointed to her cast.

"I am sorry to hear you broke your foot, but I want you to know recht away I did not ask to meet with you for your sympathy," Priscilla said sharply.

"I didn't come to get yours either. I came as the nurse to examine you, because I and many other people close to you are worried about your health. That's all." Hal pulled her stethoscope out of her nurse bag, examined Priscilla and put it back away. "Now how are you feeling?"

Priscilla blushed as she looked at her lap. "I do not hurt much anymore down there. That is gute I think."

"The bruising and swelling is gone which is gute. You hurt emotionally more than physically. I can see that. Priscilla, you need to work your way through this terribly traumatic event and get back to living your life." Priscilla's head shot up. She glared at Hal. "If you don't, the man that assaulted you has won. Life will become better in time if you let it. Trust me when I tell you it will take time for you to regain your trust in others, but you have gute instincts. You need to rebuild feelings of being safe and trusting people. You have a gute network of family and friends that want to help you. Your self worth is damaged. The first thing to do is start somewhere. Like coming downstairs to eat with your family."

"I cannot," Priscilla said obstinately.

"You don't want sympathy you said. So here is my opinion. Don't do it for yourself. Think of your mother. You were a gute helper to her for this family. She has plenty to do without waiting on you hand and foot when you don't need it. You said you aren't sick physically."

Priscilla said meekly, "I am not. Not really."

"Gute to hear you say so. Now you have to work on your emotional needs. Start by walking out of this room. Once you are comfortable eating with your family, you can help redd up the kitchen after meals. Walk out on the porch to get fresh air and sunlight. You're looking pale. Sunlight will be gute for you. Take it from there one step at a time. Go for a walk to get exercise." Nurse Hal nonchalantly added the last comment. "Let Bobby come and see you."

That was more advice than Priscilla wanted. "I do not want to see Bobby. Now I am tired. I'm going to my room."

"Fine, I need to get home before my baby wakes up, wanting to eat, but I will be back," Hal vowed to Priscilla's back.

On the way home, Emma said she wished Priscilla could come back to work since she was going to deliver soon.

Hal said, "That may not happen any time soon if ever. She'd be uneasy in the shop even though going back to work would be gute for her. If she stayed busy, she'd keep her mind off what happened.

In the meantime have Adam change things around to make the shop look different just in case Priscilla changes her mind. That might help. Move those birdhouses from behind the counter so she doesn't have to turn her back to the door.

Maybe you can offer to spend several days at the shop with her until she gets used to coming and going again. That might ease the transition for her."

"Jah, I will change the way the shop looks since Adam is so busy. My offer to stay with Priscilla until she is comfortable sounds like a gute idea." Emma let out a long sigh. "If she will only agree to come back to work."

"I didn't mean for you to take on the task," Hal grouched.

"The bird houses are not heavy. Moving them will not be a burden on me. If that makes a difference with how Priscilla feels, it is the least I can do for her," Emma declared.

The next afternoon a buggy drove in at the Lapp farm. Biscuit howled fit to be tied. Nora looked out the living room window and told Hal the company was Bobby Keim. She went to the door to greet him.

Bobby took his straw hat off and kept his head downcast. "I have come to see Nurse Hal." He looked uncomfortable about the coming conversation.

"Wilcom, Bobby. I've been waiting for your visit," Hal

called from the couch.

Bobby hung his straw hat on a peg and came to her. As soon as Nora brought a chair from the kitchen, she left.

"Sit down, Bobby." The young man did as Hal told him. "I know how hard this is to talk about with me, but I wanted to visit with you before you see Priscilla."

Bobby rubbed his forehead like he was getting a headache. "I cannot understand why this terrible thing happened to Priscilla. Do you suppose her attacker was a man she dated in the past like others say? Did she lead him on some time , and he wanted to get even?"

"Nah, and I'd hoped you weren't thinking that way. You must get those thoughts out of your head. You cannot bring them up to Priscilla. She isn't to blame for this vile crime. A sick man hurt her. He's a man that's a repeat offender and needs to be caught. It's going to take that young woman time to get over what happened to her. What she's going through is the way any woman would feel in her place. She needs everyone's patience with her," Hal lectured.

"I want to see her. Has she ask for me?" Bobby asked.

"Nah, but you should see her. I want to be sure your visit goes well. Recht now Priscilla is nervous enough around Emma and me. She'll be very nervous with you just because you're a man and are her special friend," Hal explained.

Bobby looked stunned. "Why would she feel that way? We have become close. She knows I want to marry her."

Hal said, "Priscilla feels guilty and ashamed for what happened. She hasn't a reason to feel that way, but she does. You have to make sure you don't act like you blame her. Don't ask her questions. Reassure her you will help her when she needs you and listen to her when she tells you how she feels. You have to take this slow until Priscilla feels better."

"All recht, I understand," Bobby agreed.

"Recht now, I'm not sure how she'll receive you, but Emma went into Priscilla's bedroom, knowing she wasn't welcomed. She got Priscilla to talk to her. Recently, Priscilla came downstairs to let me check her health, because I couldn't climb the stairs. Emma and I believe it might be worth a try for you to visit her. Once she's over the awkwardness of your confronting her, she might calm down. If she doesn't, you must leave recht away and try again later. If she does let you stay, don't push her and don't stay long. Talk small talk about the weather, your mother, calving, Adam and Emma or what you've been doing. Wait for Priscilla to confide in you. Remember she needs time."

"Jah, I understand." Bobby stood up and went for his hat." I will give it a try, and let you know how the visit went."

Bobby was so eager to see Priscilla he went that afternoon. He told Polly Nurse Hal said he should try to see Priscilla in her room if Polly thought it was all recht.

Polly hesitated. "I keep hoping for something to cause a turn around in Priscilla. Maybe you are that turn around. My girl is not receiving company so please do not upset her too much."

"Nurse Hal warned me about that. I will leave recht away if I must," Bobby said earnestly.

With heavy feet, he climbed the stairs. A sweat broke out on his forehead as he walked to Priscilla's closed door. He knocked so she'd know he was there and wiped his perspiring face on his long sleeve.

Priscilla called, "Who is it?"

Not taking a chance Priscilla would refuse him sight unseen, Bobby opened the door wide and removed his hat. "It is me."

Her face flushed as she scolded, "I told my mother not to let you up here if you dared to come. Go way, Bobby Keim."

Bobby moved the hat in a circle with his hands. "I have been worried about you. I want you to know how much I love you and miss you something awful. You should not feel guilty about what happened?"

Priscilla bristled up, ready for an argument. "What makes you think that is how I feel? Do you think I let that man do what he did to me? He beat me for fighting him until my face has been unrecognizable for days. I passed out from the pain. I am an innocent victim. You should just leave." She tried not to flinch under Bobby's penetrating gaze.

Bobby's scrutiny never wavered as he studied her. A thought suddenly hit him, leaving him weak in the knees. He realized there was a chasm as wide as the gap between the banks of Bender Creek at its widest. Was this gap too wide for him to bring her back to him?

"If that is the way you want it, I will go. Should you change your mind, you let me know. I will wait to hear from you," Bobby said.

Priscilla swallowed hard and nodded to show she'd heard him before she looked away. She didn't have it in her to watch Bobby's sagging shoulders as he walked away from her and out of her life.

Chapter 12

The last of July, Priscilla realized she was pregnant when she suffered from morning sickness and no longer had her monthly. Without explaining why, on one of Emma's visits, Priscilla told Emma she wanted to see Nurse Hal. On her way home, Emma stopped by the Lapp farm and arranged to pick up Hal for a house call at the Tefertiller farm.

The next morning was suitable to both of them. Hal's parents and Tootie had moved to their homes. Hal sent Daniel over to ask her mother and aunt to come stay with the baby.

As soon as Emma knocked on the Tefertiller door, Polly opened it. She whispered, "Priscilla is waiting in the living room for you, Nurse Hal."

Emma and Hal gave each other a surprised look. This was a first and maybe a positive moment. The young woman came downstairs on her own.

Priscilla was on the couch, waiting for Hal. Nurse Hal sat down by her and put her nursing bag between them. "Emma said you wanted me to check on you. How are you doing?"

Priscilla's voice was full of trauma as she stared at her clasped hands. "What happened to me has become a living nightmare. I wake not being able to breathe. I feel that man on me, holding me to the floor and laughing at me. Even though I passed out.

The fear of that awful time is so strong I'm afraid to sleep until I doze off from weariness. Even my own bedroom does not feel safe to me. I am startled by every little noise. What am I going to do? I do not think I will ever get my peace of mind back."

Hal said, "You will. It takes time, but you will. You might stop thinking so much about what happened to you if you spent your time constructively. Why don't you go back to work for Adam? Emma isn't going to be able to watch the shop much longer. She will deliver soon."

"Nah, going back to the shop to work recht now is not going to happen as much as work might be gute for me. I cannot do that." Tears sprang to Priscilla's eyes as she lowered her voice, "I had a reason for asking you to come. I want whatever kind of medicine you can give me that causes a woman to lose a baby. Mama says there are such things. She thinks you would have the recht portions to be effective. Strong and still yet safe for me to take like rhubarb and pepper mixed with laudanum or a strong tansy tea."

Hal listened intently. "I see. I've never known the portions of those concoctions. Just heard about them. You telling me you're pregnant?"

Priscilla nodded.

"You know it's against Amish beliefs to take a human life. You need to give serious thought to what you're planning," Hal suggested. "I'll not help you take this baby's life when it wasn't the baby's fault how it was conceived. Surely if you cannot raise your baby, we can find a couple to adopt the baby and love it."

Priscilla stood up. "No matter how strong the Amish belief is, sometimes there are reasons nochcoomer (off-spring) are unexpected and unwanted. This is one of those times. Since you cannot help me I am going back to my room. Denki for your taking the trouble to come see me."

On the way home, Hal was so quiet Emma had to ask how the visit went.

Not wanting to divulge too much about what Priscilla told her, Hal surmised, "I don't know if Priscilla will ever to pull herself out of what has happened and go on living. You shouldn't expect too much from her."

"It is so sad, Hallie. I have always thought of her as being like a feisty unbroken colt instead of the way she is now. I was not fond of her until she settled down, and Bobby took notice of her. They seemed so recht together as a couple. I had such hopes for their happiness. Now she is like a beaten mare with her spirit broken. I wish I could do more for her."

"Emma, you did all you can do. You must start thinking about yourself now. What happens next is up to Priscilla. I can tell you it might not be a gute idea for Bobby to visit her unless she asks for him," Hal said.

*   *   *

Emma stopped at the Keim farm on the way home. She found Bobby in the barn graining his work horses. She passed the message on to him that another visit wouldn't help the way Priscilla felt. She was too withdrawn right now. It would be better if he stayed away from Priscilla.

Bobby hated to hear that. He didn't want to give up trying just yet. He had to make one more try to get through to Priscilla. The next morning he drove to the Tefertiller farm and insisted he had to see Priscilla. Polly didn't bother to go upstairs and ask Priscilla. She told Bobby to go to her daughter's room and even wished him gute luck though she knew his visit would end hopelessly.

Priscilla heard Bobby's voice downstairs talking to her mother. Her heart pounded in her chest as she listened to his footsteps on the stairs. She sat up in bed and tucked the Trip Around The World quilt around her, hiding her whole body so he couldn't see the bulge in her middle.

Bobby pushed the door open and stepped in without knocking.

"Bobby?" Her heart melted when she saw the changes that had came over him. Dark shadows under his eyes and his haggard face made him look much older. She hated to see him suffering because of her.

"I couldn't wait any longer to come see you again. I am sorry if I said the wrong things the last time we talked," he said, twisting his straw hat in his hands. "It is hard for me to know exactly how to talk to you. I need you to know I can helped you through this for both our sakes. We need to be together."

"Nah, you could not help me. No one can, because no one knows how I feel," Priscilla stated matter of factually.

"Maybe we have to leave this to God to help you feel better. Sure enough, I need you to know I am here for you." Bobby stared at the hat in his hands as he leaned against the wall to help hold himself up.

Priscilla shook her head as she tried to keep her voice emotionless. "You need to move on and find someone to love. I want you to be happy, and that cannot be with me. I have not a happy future in front of me. Now go away. I mean it when I say I do not want you to come back."

Bobby believed her now. He gave up trying to convince her. He was out of words. He jammed his straw hat on his head and left.

Priscilla rolled on her side and faced the wall. No way could she blot out the sound of Bobby's heavy farmer shoes as he tromped downstairs. It was as if he had lead weights tied to his feet.

Soft falling rain trickled down the bedroom window pane like angel tears. Her eyes burned just thinking about it. They could cry all they wanted. She wouldn't join them. At the moment, she didn't have any tears left to cry.

On Emma's next visit Priscilla said dully, "Bobby came again. You must make him understand he has to leave me alone."

"If that is what you want, I will tell him for you. For what it is worth as your friend, I believe you are making a mistake to let go of the best man you will ever meet," Emma said.

"Lately, I have not gotten anything I want so why should that change now?" Priscilla spit out bitterly. "This is the way it has to be. I suppose Nurse Hal told you about her visit with me?"

"Nah, Hallie does not discuss her patients with me. It is not permitted," Emma said.

"Let me tell you why Bobby cannot come back. I am expecting a baby. No man should want to have anything to do with such as me now. This sure enough makes me second hand goods, ain't so?" Priscilla asked.

"Did you tell Bobby this?" Emma spotted the dull guilt in the woman's eyes. "You did not tell Bobby about the baby. You are wrong to keep this from him. He needs to know. It is his choice to make if he wants to marry you now."

"You may be recht, but I just cannot face him with that news," Priscilla said stubbornly.

"Let Bobby decide if he can handle knowing about the baby," Emma insisted. "You will make the biggest mistake of your life if you do not give Bobby a chance to show you how much he loves you."

"Go home, Emma. I do not want to talk anymore," Priscilla said.

On her way home, Emma's stopped at Bishop Bontrager's house to tell him Priscilla needed his counseling. Elton told her it was time he talked to Priscilla.

Polly greeted the bishop and his wife at the door. "Come in. It is nice to see both of you. Might I get you a cup of coffee?"

Bishop Bontrager said, "Sure enough, Jane might like a cup and a visit with you. Your daughter, Priscilla, has not been to church since what happened at Keim's Furniture Shop. It is my duty as bishop to visit her."

"You are welcome to try. Priscilla does not see visitors except for Emma Keim and Nurse Hal. Go upstairs. Priscilla's room is the second door on the recht," Polly told him. As the bishop took the stairs, Polly said, "Now, Jane, let's have that coffee."

Jane patted Polly's hand. "First, let us pray Elton is able to help Priscilla."

The bishop knocked on the closed door. "Priscilla Tefertiller, this is Bishop Bontrager. Might I have a few words with you?"

Priscilla's muffled voice came through the door so soft she was hard to hear. "Bishop, come in."

Elton found her in bed, covered up to her chin. "You do not look like someone expecting visitors. Are you very sick?"

Priscilla sat up and put her pillow behind her back. "I am not sick. I do not have visitors often so there is no need to get out of bed. No one I want to see."

Elton narrowed his eyes at her. "Does that include me?"

"Jah, I cannot imagine why you want to bother with me anyway," Priscilla said truthfully.

"You are a member of the Amish community. That makes you as important to me, the bishop, as any other member. You have missed quite a few worship services. It is not permitted to miss worship for very long unless you are ill," the bishop said. "You just said it is not because of sickness. So what is your excuse?"

"You know what happened to me at the furniture shop. Does that not sound like enough to make me not want to face anyone?" Priscilla asked.

"Tell me why you think this is so?"

"For several reasons. I expect at the worship services and the women's gatherings I am called second hand goods. I do not know how I can ever face them again, knowing what they think of me. I might even be bad for Adam's business if I went back to work.

Tell me, Bishop, what am I to think? I remember that sermon you gave about Diana Kingman. Halt dich frei fuhn manslet. You said that. Keep yourself free from men. Remember the message about if our reputations are lost we can only regain them at a dreadful cost?"

"Now talk fershtendich (sensible) once. Diana Kingman did not keep herself free from men. You are different. The bible says, *'But if a man finds a betrothed damsel in the field, and the man forces her, and lies with her then the man only that lay with her shall die.'* What I am saying to you is you are not to blame for what happened to you. You were taken by force. You must not forsake God by staying away from worship services just when you need his help the most.

In Hebrews is the verse, *'Now faith is the substance of things hoped for, the evidence of things not seen.'* By that I am telling you to have enough faith in God to come to the worship services, because faith is the evidence of a gute thing not seen by you that will surely happen.

What happens to you from now on is God's will. Our Lord sure enough did not mean for you to waste your life in this bed. You are young and have a stronger nature than that, ain't so?" the bishop said bluntly. He added, "It might help your outlook on life if you forgive your attacker."

Priscilla said testily, "After how he ruined my life, I do not feel I can do that."

"Sunday, the members sat through a worship service where Preacher Yoder and I lectured them on the value of helping those that need it.

You will find facing the community easier than you suppose it to be. I do expect to see you with your family in two weeks at the worship service unless you want to be shunned for not attending. I will have no choice but to bring you up before a member meeting for a vote on this matter," the bishop stated.

Priscilla's face paled. "You are making this so very hard for me, Bishop. There is more you do not know. I am going to have a baby because of what happened to me. Soon I will show enough that everyone would notice. You tell me now how I am supposed to face people? It is hard enough just to face my family and Emma."

Bishop Bontrager folded his arms over his chest and narrowed his eyes. "You start by doing so and see what happens. You will be surprised to see how everyone will welcome you at Gemeesunndaag services. I am sorry to hear your life has been made more difficult.

For recht now, you start by attending worship services. You have to stay recht with God. Pray for His guidance and let him answer your prayers. In the meantime, you are not alone. Your loving parents and siblings want to help so stop shutting them out. Loyal friends, Emma and Adam Keim, are available to lean on. That is a start. Now I am going to leave you to think about all I said."

After he left, Priscilla went over in her mind what the bishop told her. She didn't want to be shunned. She went downstairs and asked her mother to send one of her brothers with a message to Bobby Keim. She wanted to talk to him recht away. For this meeting, she made the effort to be in the living room when he arrived. If he'd accept her while she was pregnant with her attacker's baby, she'd agree to marry him.

When Bobby arrived an hour later, Priscilla took a deep breath. "Please sit down so we can talk. Recht away I must say I do not feel I did anything wrong to cause what happened to me, Bobby."

"I believe you did not," Bobby said earnestly.

"If you do, I am grateful. Does anyone else in this community believe what happened was not my fault?" Priscilla asked.

Bobby shrugged. "All I know is those that talks to me are worried about you. They miss you at worship services and the singings. Adam misses your help at the shop, and Emma will not be able to help at the shop in a matter of a few days. She wishes you would come back to work.

I miss keeping company with you and our talks about the future. Come join me at the worship services and singings. You can see for yourself how people feel about you. You will know I am telling the truth."

Priscilla broke into tears. "Bishop Bontrager came to see me today. He gave me no choice. I have to come to worship services or be brought up before a member meeting to be shunned. I just wish it was that simple. This facing everyone. Bobby, you must know I love you and miss you. As hard as this is for me to say, I cannot go anywhere or think about marrying you until you hear what I have to tell you."

"I can help you endure the anguish you are going through. Just let me. As time goes by you will feel better with God's help. I am sure of that," Bobby said.

Priscilla put a hand on his arm to stop him. "Listen to me. I have to tell you this, and it needs said. I am having the baby of that awful man who raped me. The baby is due sometime in November."

Bobby leaned his deflated back against the couch and stared at his hands. "Are you sure?"

Priscilla nodded. "Jah, Nurse Hal has been here. She said I am . You can see it would not be fair to marry you now if you are not comfortable with an unwanted baby. I will not blame you if you leave now, Bobby, and do not come back. I wish this was not so. Emma insisted I tell you the truth so there you have it. You might just want to give me space to grieve for what we had, and time to have a baby I do not want until after November. I would understand."

"Did you ever stop to think you should give me a choice in this?" Bobby looked hurt.

"Do you want to marry me now that I am second hand goods with a baby on the way?"

"I need time to think. I do love you, Priscilla." Bobby stood and put his hat on. "I want to think about what is best for the two of us."

Bobby walked out the front door and closed it. Watching the man she loved walk away from her was his answer. Surely this last time she might ever talk to Bobby was the hardest one of the trials she'd faced.

Emma made a visit to Priscilla a couple days later. First, Priscilla told her about Bishop Bontrager's visit, and his ultimatum that she go to worship services or be shunned.

"I am so sorry. I did not think he would push you so hard." Emma felt guilty about talking to the bishop.

Priscilla shrugged as she told Emma about her meeting with Bobby. As she expected, she wasn't surprised by his reaction, she told Emma, "When he found out she was pregnant. He left. I am three months along now. I asked Nurse Hal for a remedy for a miscarriage, because I do not want this baby. She refused to help me."

Emma placed her hands on her expanding stomach. "No baby should be unwanted. A baby is put in this world by God and should be loved even if that baby is here only a short time."

"How will I ever look at this baby and not remember how I came by it?" Priscilla asked sharply.

"Your motherly instincts will kick in when you hold the baby. It will be your baby," Emma insisted.

"That is fine for you to say, but I do not know that it will be that way. Maybe if the baby is a girl and looks like me, I might feel more loving toward it." She paused a moment. "Nah, Nurse Hal should have helped me get rid of the baby. It is just one more problem for me that is going to ruin my life with Bobby," Priscilla moaned.

"Hallie is not the type of nurse that would harm an unborn baby. I am glad she did not help you. Babies are precious gifts. Everyone of them. That baby did not ask to be given parents that did not want him or her. You have no recht to push your revenge off on an innocent little baby and take its life," Emma stormed.

"It is not my shoes you are walking in when you preach to me. Remember that," Priscilla sassed stubbornly.

Emma felt her temper rising. "How about you try walking in my shoes for me? I am having twins. One of my babies is not going to live unless God sees fit to create a miracle for me. The baby has a hole in his heart and brain damage. A prayer circle is on going recht now. One of the largest ever heard of, praying for this baby to live and be able to grow up with his twin sister. He is loved by Adam and me and the whole extended family, but that is not enough. The baby is in God's hands. We have to live with what is God's will. You are having a healthy baby that will thrive with love from you. That makes you a lucky mother. Do not tell me to walk in your shoes unless you are willing to walk in mine."

Tears streamed down Emma's face as she rushed across the living room and left the house.

With her hands over her face, Priscilla cried out, "What have I done? I didn't mean to upset Emma. I did not know what she and Adam are going through. She should have told me before this already."

Part of Nurse Hal's advice was to get outside. Maybe that would help her outlook. Priscilla got up and walked out on the porch. She'd always loved summer. The warm breeze played at her dress and apron.

She hadn't heard the birds twitter in the eaves for months. So many sights she'd missed out on in while she holed up in her room. Like the chickens over by the barn, racing after a grasshopper. The rooster crowing and hens cackling.

Look how much the spring calves had grown already. They were a good size, trying to keep up with the stock cows on their path to the pond for a drink. The mares had foaled without her there to watch them. So much that awful man took away from her that made her give up on life for all those months.

The milk cows headed for the barn, bawling that they were coming to be milked. So many sights and sounds she loved to see and hear.

She plopped down in a rocker to think. Watching Emma and Bobby walk away from her was a gigantic wake up call. The bishop's warning he'd have her shunned by the community was another one.

At supper, she announced to her family she wanted to go to the next worship service with them. The bishop had given her no choice. He'd bring her name up at the member meeting if she didn't attend.

It wasn't fair to her family to put them all through the difficult days during a shunning. She'd eat at a small table next to the family table. No one could speak to her or look at her. Most of the time the punishment lasted six weeks, and the bishop would tell her he wanted her to kneel and ask for forgiveness in front of a member meeting to stop the shunning.

Sunday morning was one of the most nerve racking times Priscilla and her family could ever remember in their lives. Polly walked into Jonas Stolfus's house beside Priscilla. They sat on an empty bench behind other women.

Emma kept glancing over her shoulder and finally spotted Priscilla. She patted Hal's arm and nodded toward the Tefertiller women.

Hal whispered in Emma's ear. They stood up and walked back to sit by Priscilla and Polly.

After the worship service, Priscilla got many welcome back hugs. The women made an effort to put her and her family at ease.

Chapter 13

The next morning, Emma redded up the kitchen. After she finished, she sat down in her rocker. She rubbed her stomach to let the babies know she was thinking about them as she closed her eyes to pray. "Lord, you will have to give Adam and me the strength to take whatever your will is for these babies. Please help us to remain strong no matter what you decide, but know if you let both our babies live, we will love them and care for them in your name. Amen."

For most of the morning, Emma rocked and prayed. Finally, she opened her eyes and glanced at the wall clock. She should fix lunch to take to Adam at the shop. It wouldn't do her or the babies any good to waste away her day in that rocker.

Before she left the house she picked up the tear gas canister Hallie gave her and put it in her apron pocket. She felt paranoid carrying around that canister and locking her doors, but everyone kept telling her to be safe.

It was such a good day to walk, Emma decided to cut across the timber. The thick tree growth supplied cool shade which brought a breeze that felt good.

A bible verse popped in her head. She stopped walking and said loudly, "This is the day the Lord has made. We will rejoice and be glad in it."

The sound of her voice disturbed a flock of sparrows in the tree above her. They left the limbs rocking and the leaves shaking as they flew away. "I probably did not make the birds and animals in this timber want to rejoice," Emma said.

When the humming noise began around her face and hands, Emma wasn't so sure a walk in the woods was a good idea. She had forgotten the mosquitoes. Pulling her bonnet tight on her head, she tied the strings to keep the insects from slipping in. The rest of the way to the meadow, she waved her hands around her face to keep from getting bit too many times.

By the time Emma arrived at the shop with enough lunch for two, she'd made up her mind she wasn't wasting the rest of this day. She told Adam she wanted to clerk at the shop that afternoon if he needed to go on a job. She couldn't sit around and do nothing and feel sad. She needed to keep busy.

Her practical husband wrote on his pad, "You should stay home where it is safer and rest like Hal said."

Emma shook her head. "I can sit down and rest recht here when I am tired unless you are afraid that would turn one of your rockers into used furniture." She thought teasing would make Adam's smile, but he didn't find her joke funny. So she tried another tack. "I can do a few necessary things that do not take much energy. The merchandise is in need of a gute dusting, and the kerosene lamp bases need filled. Those are not taxing jobs."

Adam consented on his pad. "All recht, but do not get overly tired." He put his pad away and got it back out. "Stay alert! I do not think it is safe here for you."

"Stop worrying. I have the tear gas in my apron pocket, but I do not expect to be attacked here like Priscilla. That man would have to be a dummkopf to come back to the same spot again," Emma declared.

After Adam left, Emma put the chimneys on the shelf behind the counter which was now empty. The birdhouses were on a shelf on a side wall. After she took the lamps apart, she the lined the bases up on the counter and came around in front. She'd set the small kerosene can on the floor. The small spout was made to stick in the base openings. In no time, she had three of the bases filled and two more to go. Smiling, she thought to herself that she'd soon work herself out of easy jobs and get to sit in one of Adam's new rockers.

A voice behind her said, "Hello there."

Emma turned around to welcome a customer, wondering how she could concentrate so hard she didn't hear the door bell. Her smile dried up. The young Englisher, with the red car, was holding the bell above the door so it wouldn't jingle.

"What do you want?" Emma snapped, immediately on guard.

He sauntered toward her, pulling a folded pillow case out of his jacket pocket. "Surprised that I came back, Sweety. I hoped I'd be lucky enough to find you here this time. You can't imagine my disappointment when I found another woman working here in your place. You know I had a hunch the other clerk might not be ready to come back to work yet after that fun time we had."

Her back against the counter, Emma froze with a kerosene bowl in her shaking hands. She looked out the window, wondering why she hadn't heard a car motor. The car wasn't in front of the store. She put her concentration on the man edging at her, smiling his crooked grin as he unfolded the pillow case. He reminded her a tom cat sneaking up on an unsuspecting mouse. No matter what she wasn't going to let him harm the babies inside her.

"Awe, come on. We should be able to get along now that we know each other so well," he said, his smile turning to a sneer.

"You leave recht now. It will not work to harm me. You were not able to get the pillow case over my head. I saw your face so I can tell the sheriff what you look like," Emma said.

His eyes narrowed as he focused on her. "Well, well, I guess it doesn't make much difference to me whether your head is covered or not as long as I get what I came for. I don't figure on you being able to talk by the time I'm done with you. After all, I've waited most of a year to catch you alone." He glanced around the room and backed over to the work shop door, daring her to run. "You are alone, aren't you?"

"Only for a few minutes. My husband is coming any minute," Emma lied.

The man opened the door and checked for Adam in the

work shop. He closed the door. "Good, we're alone. I promise all I need is a few minutes of your time."

Emma had to come up with a plan quick. The man was telling the truth. He couldn't afford to leave the shop with her alive. She couldn't go behind the counter. He'd corner her like he did Priscilla. With the lamp base still gripped tightly in her hand, she waited and watched him come at her. "I do not know you. What is your name?"

His voice was enough to threaten Emma to the core. "No harm in telling you since we're going to become so imminently acquainted. My name is Scott Lang."

The whiff of cigarette smoke and cologne was strong on the man as he closed in on Emma.

Please help me, Lord. She slung the glass base at his face. Kerosene splashed in his eyes and spread over his face.

Lang squalled in pain like a cat that a horse stepped on, and mashed its tail. He swore words at her Emma hoped she never had an opportunity to hear again as he sheltered his face and eyes in his soft hands. Shaking his head, he bent over double, unable to see.

Emma slipped passed him and looked for something to hit him with. Close by was an umbrella stand filled with decorative, wooden walking canes. She picked up one. Holding it like a baseball bat, she smacked the man in the back of his head as if he was the baseball, and she meant to make a home run. The man fell forward from the blow. He hit the front of his head on the counter, making a smacking sound on contact. He flopped onto the floor, unconscious.

As Emma ran across the room, something in her apron pocket bumped against her leg. She remembered the tear gas she hadn't used. She hadn't needed it this time, but, God forbid, she'd remember it next time if she had to use it on him in a few minutes. She rushed out the door. The red car wasn't sitting anywhere in sight. That pervert had thought of everything. He hid the car so people traveling on the road wouldn't see it.

What was she going to do? She'd walked to work so she didn't have a buggy to get away fast in. This man seemed to know her well enough that he may know where she lived. He'd be mad enough to come after her or catch up with her in the timber on the way home. He wouldn't be out cold for long.

Bobby! He might be working around home. She'd cut through the field of shocks to the Keim house. For sure, Lovina would be home. She'd hide with her mother-in-law. Maybe the man wouldn't think to look there. If Bobby was home, he could go to the phone shed and call the sheriff.

Emma walked as fast as she could which wasn't very fast given her unbalanced posture. She batted at a persistent deer fly buzzing on her neck below her prayer cap. The fly's closeness gave her goose bumps as he tried to land.

As she made her way through the rough field, she saw the red car hidden between two of the large, golden oat shocks. The man would surely head her direction when he came to for no other reason than to get his car. She had to hurry.

Emma made it half way across the field and stopped to rest. Her breath came out in fast puffs as her lungs felt like they might burst. Breathing that hard made her fuzzy headed. She willed herself not to pass out from all this exertion before she found Bobby or Lovina.

She had to stop for a moment. Emma's leg muscles were on fire, but she couldn't rest for long. She paused to catch her breath and glance over her shoulder. No sign of the man. If only he stayed unconscious until the sheriff arrived. "I hope that awful man has two big goose eggs on his head that gives him a headache for a long time." She knew how awful that sounded even to herself. She looked at the cloudless, blue sky above her. "Sorry, God, I am just not in a forgiving mood at this moment."

She checked the glaring sun slanted in the western sky. Time must be between two and three. She increased her pace to the field gate. Adam and his brother made tight fences and gates. She struggled to pull the number nine wire off the wooden post with the barbed wire wrapped around it. Finally, she succeeded, walked through and closed the gate.

Ahead of her were the Keim farm buildings and house. A feeling of safety calmed her some what as she headed for the house. Behind her, a man shouted, "Emma!"

She about jumped out of her skin as she whirled around. Seeing Bobby in the barn door made her knees wobble in relief. Her head swirled, and she felt like she was going to sink to the ground.

Adam's brother rushed toward her. "Emma, what is wrong? Is it your time?"

Emma struggled to tell him between panting about the man, and how he came to be lying on the shop floor. He meant to attack her. The man admitted he attacked Priscilla. Bobby became angry when she said, "Please, go call the sheriff to come quick. I am afraid Adam will walk in on that man. He is dangerous. He said he intended to kill me since I saw his face."

Bobby's face turned red as he growled, "I will take care of him myself for what he did to Priscilla and wanted to do to you. The sheriff can have him after I am through with him. You go in the house and stay with Mama. Lock the doors."

"Bobby, nah, not you. I know the man is dangerous. You will get hurt. Go call the sheriff please," Emma begged.

Bobby turned his back on her and ran toward the oat field, retracing Emma's steps.

Emma burst into the kitchen. Lovina, a thin woman with more gray in her hair than black, turned from the stove. One look at her disheveled and panting daughter-in-law made her ask, "Was ist letz?"

Her knees threatening to buckle, Emma grabbed for a chair and plopped down. She told her story again as fast as she could. "I am afraid for Bobby, Lovina. He would not listen when I asked him to go call the sheriff. He is determined to go after that man on his own because of what the man did to Priscilla. I am afraid he will be hurt, and Adam is due home soon. He might be hurt, too. That man is so dangerous. He intended to kill me. I begged Bobby to call the sheriff, but he just wouldn't listen. Why would he not listen?" She burst into tears.

"First, we are going to get you in bed, Emma Keim. You have had too much excitement and stress. You have to think about your babies," Lovina ordered.

"Nah, I have to go back as soon as I catch my breath. If I

had known how mad Bobby would be at that awful man, I would not have told him. I should have gone to the phone shed myself," Emma declared.

"You go to bed and rest. I will make the call to the sheriff," Lovina said. Emma opened her mouth to protest, but Lovina scolded, "You have not the strength to do otherwise."

"But you should not be alone in plain sight as long as that man is on the loose," Emma protested.

"He will not bother me. After what you did to him, he will be ready to leave before someone catches him if Bobby has not already," Lovina assured her as she dawned her bonnet.

Emma gave up and headed to the bedroom.

Lovina hurried out the kitchen door. She harnessed a horse to the small one seat buggy, hopped in and flipped the lines on the horse's back so he'd trot. The closest place was the Jostle farm. She didn't see any reason to go any further. The phone shed was farther away in the opposite direction. It would take the sheriff too long to get here from Wickenburg. Action needed to be taken fast to help Bobby and maybe Adam.

Lovina pulled back on the lines to slow the horse down to make the turn into the Jostle driveway. She headed for the house and barn. Jake Jostle, a surly, lanky, sun browned man, came out of the barn.

At first sight of Jake, Lovina was nervous about talking to the unfriendly man she usually avoided at worship services. *You have to do this,* she told herself. *This is an emergency.* She shook the lines to hurry the horse.

While she kept her eyes on Jake Jostle, she didn't see the flock of hens scratching in the road. The horse ran into their midst. The chickens squawked as they flew up around the horse, causing him to rear up. Lovina feared he was going to flip over backward on her. She screamed, causing the horse to put all four hooves back on the driveway and race toward the barn.

"Help me! Help," she cried.

Jake's three sons, all patterned after him with that lanky, gangling Jostle stature, came out of the barn to stand by Jake. When they saw Lovina was in trouble, they dropped their carpenter tools and raced toward her buggy. Jake and Albert stepped into the driveway in front of the horse, waving their arms and crying whoa. Will and Sam got on each side of the horse and caught the harness. The boys skidded along with the horse until he slowed and stopped. He stood, looking wild eyed as he shuddered and panted.

After scattering Jostle's chickens, Jake's frowning face made Lovina worry he wouldn't help her. She looked back to see if she had left any feathered bodies in the driveway. Nah, she missed all the hens. That gave her some relief.

Pale faced and shaking like a leaf in a stiff wind, Lovina wilted in the seat.

Jake gripped the side of the buggy seat and asked, "Was ist letz?"

"Something terrible has happened. I need help. My daughter-in-law was attacked at the shop by the man that hurt Priscilla Tefertiller," Lovina said quickly.

Albert said snidely, "Sure enough! There will not be any need for the sheriff to think I am guilty anymore, ain't so?"

"Enough, son. Be quiet and listen to Lovina Keim," Jake snapped. "Was Emma Keim hurt?"

"Nah, she got away from the man and came to my house. She asked my son, Bobby, to go call the sheriff. He has been upset over what happened to Priscilla Tefertiller. Emma says Bobby took it on himself to go to Adam's shop after the man. The man is dangerous and strong enough to kill, and Bobby surely will need help. Adam is due home soon, but that might not be soon enough to help Bobby. That means Adam would be in danger," Lovina rambled and stopped for breath. "Can you help my son?"

"We will help him. That man has to be stopped. You go in the house and stay with my wife. You are safe here," Jake said.

Lovina shook her head. "Ach, denki, but I cannot stay. That awful Englisher frightened Emma Keim so much that I have her in bed at my place. She has not been well for some time. I have to go back and take care of her. Recht now she is alone and frightened the man might come in on her."

"All recht, let Will and Sam ride back in the buggy with

you. Albert and I will ride the work horses to the shop to help Bobby Keim. Will, you let Lovina Keim out of the buggy and go on to the phone shed as fast as you can. Call the sheriff and explain what has happened. Afterwards, the two of you come back to Lovina's and stay with the women. If that man gets away, she and Emma Keim will need your protection," Jake ordered.

Lovina gladly offered Will the lines as she scooted over to let the two boys sit with her. "Denki, I am too shaky to drive."

Will took the lines and turned the horse around.

In a few minutes, Jake and Albert raced their golden draft horses down the road and passed the buggy. They pulled into the Keim driveway, jumped off the work horses at the hitch rail and tied the reins.

They turned around fast as the shop door slammed. A stranger, a well dressed but disheveled Englisher, ran right at them. Jake and Albert tackled him head on and brought him to the ground. As he struggled and cursed, Jake tied his arms and legs with the two pieces of baling twine he'd put in his trouser pocket.

"Sit on him, Albert. I will go check on Bobby Keim," Jake ordered. Albert plopped down hard enough to knock the wind out of the loud mouthed man. That silenced him for the moment.

Jake raced to the shop and came face to face with Bobby staggering out the door. He was holding the side of his head.

"You all recht?" Jake asked, grabbing him by the shoulder.

"I will be," Bobby said, rubbing his face.

Jake thumbed over his shoulder and actually smiled. "Albert and me have the man on the ground and tied up. Will and Sam went to call the sheriff. They are going back to your house to stay with your mama and Emma Keim to protect them. All we have to do is wait for the sheriff to come get him."

"Gute," Bobby said as he kept walking toward the Englisher.

On their way back from the phone shed, Will turned the buggy into the driveway when he saw the man on the ground with Albert on his back. Adam came from the other direction and pulled in right behind him.

Jake went to meet his sons. "You boys go to Lovina Keim's house and tell her all is well here. She and Emma Keim do not have to worry anymore. The man has been caught, and Lovina's boys are unharmed. Leave Lovina's buggy by the barn and walk back home to do the chores."

Will's flipped the lines and circled the horse around Adam's carpenter wagon. Adam jumped down and trotted to where the men stood. He made a wobble with his hand to question why the man was on the ground.

Bobby and Jake took turns explaining to him the man sneaked in on Emma, planning to attack her.

Adam's eyes widened in concern.

Emma is fine. She is with Mama now," Bobby answered.

Adam wrapped his hand around Bobby's chin and shook his head. He pointed to his eye.

Jake said cheerfully, "He has a voonderball gute black eye, ain't so?"

"The Englisher has quite a punch," Bobby said, sheepishly.

Adam bent over the man and wrinkled up his nose. He waved the air in front of his face.

Bobby snickered. "Remind me to never get Emma riled and let her corner me. You should be proud of your wife. She did more damage to him than I did. She threw kerosene in his face. That's why he stinks. When he was blinded, she hit him from behind on the head with one of those wooden canes you sell. He fell forward and smacked his forehead on the counter and was out like a light. He had just came to and was about to run when I got here. We traded a few punches, before he sucker punched me and ran outside. Gute thing Jake and Albert arrived in time to stop him before he made it to his car. Emma says it is hid in the shock field."

Adam took his note pad out. He wrote, "You are sure about Emma?"

"She's all recht. She was pretty bushed and excited after she rushed across the field to the house," Bobby said.

Adam turned to Jake Jostle. He wrote on his pad. "Denki

for your help and being a gute neighbor when my family needed you."

"Sure enough, you are wilcom," Jake said.

Adam shook hands with each of the boys and patted them on the shoulder.

As soon as the sheriff left with the prisoner, Adam raced across the field with Bobby. When they arrived at the house, Lovina had supper ready. She pointed to the bedroom when Adam raised his eyebrows.

Emma was in his mother's bed with her arm over her eyes.

Adam patted her shoulder.

Slowly, she moved her arm away. "Ach! I am so glad you are here. I had such a frightful day."

Adam wrote, "You gute?"

Emma rubbed her eyes. "Jah, just tired. How about after supper we go home? I need a gute night sleep in my own bed." She sat up and threw the covers back. "Ach, I should be helping Lovina with supper."

Adam put a forefinger against her shoulder and pushed her down to the pillow.

"Lovina could use some help," Emma protested.

Adam wrote, "Mama has been fixing meals for a long time. She is an expert at it. You are going to eat in bed."

Emma opened her mouth to argue, but the I mean it look Adam gave her made her keep still. She usually held her own when she disagreed with Adam, but not when he gave her that look.

Chapter 14

Early the next morning, Hal came to the Keim farm to check on Emma. She insisted Emma go see Doctor Burns. Emma protested. She felt fine, and she had an appointment coming up in a week. Adam agreed with Hal. He went to the barn and hitched up the buggy. With that I mean it look on his face that said there wasn't any way he'd let Emma get out going, they drove to Wickenburg.

After Doctor Burns heard what she'd been through,he sent her to the hospital for another ultrasound. He asked Adam and Emma to come back to the office to wait for the results.

An hour later, Doctor Burns came to the exam room. He sat on his stool and rolled in front of Emma. "I want you to be admitted at the hospital in two days for the cesarean section. You are fine in spite of what you went through, but your due date is three weeks away. It's time to deliver the twins."

When Emma asked about the baby boy's condition, the doctor said he couldn't see any change. The outcome was still in God's hands.

Adam stopped by the Lapp farm long enough for Emma to let the family know the doctor was setting up the cesarean section. They had to increase their prayer time now and pass the word along to the rest of the prayer circle. In two days, the Keim family needed a miracle when the twins were born.

..........*

The day after the Englisher was arrested, Bishop Bontrager

and his wife, Jane, went to the Tefertiller farm to tell the family the news. Polly served them coffee and cookies until her husband, Joseph, and their two sons came to the house. Priscilla sat quietly at the end of the table, waiting to hear the reason the bishop and his wife came to visit.

When the Tefertiller family was at the table, the bishop announced the attacker showed back up at Adam Keim's furniture shop and tried to harm Emma. The man failed in his attempt, was arrested and taken to jail. Now everyone could breathe easy, including Priscilla.

Priscilla looked distressed. "That was so scary for Emma. How is she?"

"Emma was shaken up by what happened. She is having a cesarean section to deliver the babies tomorrow. We are all to pray hard the baby boy will live and be all recht," Jane answered.

Priscilla sighed. "I am glad the attacker did not harm Emma. The Keims have enough to worry about recht now. I am so sorry for what Emma and Adam are going through. Sure enough, it will be so sad for them to lose one of the babies."

Bishop Bontrager told her, "Life is about us trying to do God's will even when we do not see things his way. The Keims will be sad and grieve. All of us will grieve with them, but they are strong. They will go on with life and treasure the baby girl they still have."

"What I see in front of me is wanting to make sure that man pays for what he did to me." Priscilla's voice filled with bitterness.

Bishop narrowed his eyes at her tone. "Vengeance is mine saith the Lord. It is not your recht to repay a hateful deed as what happened to you with vengeance. You have to face what happened and move on with your life. The Englisher has won if you stay hid out as if you have already died, hating him and this baby you carry. Forgive that man for his sins, and start living again for the sake of your baby."

Jane patted Priscilla's hand. "Sure enough, you saw it was not so hard to face people at the last worship service. You are still Priscilla Tefertiller, a member of this Plain community.

Keep putting one foot in front of the other, and after while it will not be so hard to do."

Priscilla took in what they said without comment. The Bontragers couldn't tell if she took heed of their advice or not.

Bishop Bontrager asked, "Has Bobby Keim been to see you, Priscilla?"

"Jah, he has, but I am not so sure he will be back," she stated with tears in her eyes. "When he found out I was expecting a baby he left and has not been back since. He did not want to have me in his life after he heard."

Next stop that day for the bishop was the Keim farm to visit with Bobby. He wanted to find out how Bobby felt about Priscilla's problem. The couple were made to be together in the eyes of God. It would solve so much for both of them if they married and raise Priscilla's baby.

The bishop pulled up by the Keim house. Bobby came from the house to greet him. "Wilcom, come in for a cup of coffee."

The bishop smiled as he climbed down. "Nah, I will not stay long. I hear you had quite the excitement at the furniture shop. Sporting a black eye, sure enough."

"Jah, that was more excitement than I ever want to have again," Bobby said, rubbing the side of his face.

The bishop leaned against the hitch post. "I was glad when I heard Emma Keim was not harmed."

"Praise the Lord! Emma is a real fighter when cornered. She gave that Englisher a good whipping and was able to get away," Bobby bragged.

"Jah. Sometimes, I feel our Emma has too quick a temper, but I will not find fault with her this once," the bishop joked.

Bobby turned serious. "Emma is going the hospital tomorrow, but none of what takes place after the babies are born will be the fault of that vile devil."

"That is true. What happens tomorrow is God's will. Just like Priscilla Tefertiller's future is in God's hands," the bishop said. He noticed Bobby's head went up at the mention of her name. "After what that man did to her, the young woman is finally making the effort to live again beyond her bedroom walls. She needs all the comfort, understanding and help she can get from her friends, ain't so?"

"How could it be God's will that man assaulted Priscilla?" Bobby snapped.

"God did not will that terrible Englisher to assault Priscilla. I do believe what happens to her in the next few months to bring her back to a productive life or not will be God's will. How that happens for Priscilla next depends on her friends and a special friend," the bishop declared.

Bobby looked at his feet with despair in his voice. "What is it you think I should do, Bishop? I struggle, trying to decide if I can still marry Priscilla now that she is second hand goods. Can I ever forget what happened to her?"

"Bobby, I cannot tell you what to do. That has to be your decision. Nah, you can never forget what happened. Priscilla will not forget what happened. You must move on from here and pray to gather your strength from God. He will help you to make your decision. I cannot make it for you nor can Priscilla," Bishop Bontrager said.

"How do I make the recht decision? How will I know what I decide is recht?" Bobby worried.

The bishop said, "In Jeremiah, the bible says, *'Stand at the crossroads and look; ask for the ancient paths, ask where the good way is and walk in it.'* Bobby pray for God to show you the ancient path to take. One other thought I might leave with you. Remember Joseph knew that his wife, Mary, was carrying a child that was not of his making. He never once thought about turning his back on her or the baby no matter how much talk there was behind Mary's back."

"Bishop, how will I ever be able to love Priscilla's baby? Every time I look at it I will be reminded how the baby came to be," Bobby said honestly.

"Babies are not hard to love. Open your heart and love will happen. You did that once for Annie's baby. You can do it again," the bishop told him. "Now I must be headed home. I have work left undone long enough."

After the bishop left, Bobby walked behind the barn and flopped back into a hay stack. He had to give much thought to his decision, and he didn't have much time to make it. Which was the best way to go for him? Would he be able to care for and love Priscilla's baby conceived by rape? If the answer was no, could he walk away from the woman he loved and leave her to face her problems alone? Problems not of her doing. This woman is the one he wanted to spend his life with, and he really didn't want to turn his back on her. The bishop was right. He had planned to marry Annie and be the father of her baby until she was killed. Circumstances weren't so different between Annie and Priscilla. He had to admit that and make up his mind soon.

*   *   *

When Adam helped Emma into the buggy, she noticed thunderheads mound on the western horizon. A faint rumble of thunder warned her of what was to come although they faced a feeble sun. The ride to town, she usually enjoyed, seemed to take forever, measured in clip clops of the horse's hooves. Just as they reached the Wickenburg city limits, the dismal gray sky let loose a fine drizzle, coating the buggy's windshield until Adam turned the wiper on.

When Adam helped Emma from the buggy at the hospital, the drizzle misted her face. It was a miserable day. Just about as wretched as she felt.

Emma laid on the gurney, trying to numb herself to what was going to happen after the cesarean section. She knew she'd have a healthy baby girl. Doctor Burns had already promised her that much.

She felt like a proud mama every time she looked at the sonogram pictures. Baby Mary took care of her ailing brother. How hard it was going to be for Adam and her to give up the baby boy after she had carried him for almost nine months. It would be equally hard for Mary to lose her brother. Emma patted the place where she thought Joseph was in her stomach. She felt his faint kick in response.

Adam, Bobby and Lovina waited with the Lapp family in the surgery waiting room. As the time went by, Adam watched the clock hands turn so slowly.

Finally, the surgeon, Dr. Christensen, came out. He told Adam that Emma was in recovery. She was doing fine. As was expected, Emma gave birth to a healthy baby girl. She weighed five pounds which meant if she didn't have any problems developed with feeding she could go home soon.

The tiny baby boy was in critical condition. He'd be kept in the Neonatal Unit where he could be monitored. He might not live through the night, but if he did, each day that went by was encouraging. Although, he didn't want Adam and Emma to have much hope for the baby to live long. He asked Adam if he wanted to go see his babies.

Adam looked through the glass at the babies in separate incubators. He imagined Emma, as a baby, looked similar to baby Mary. Recht now, she was a very unhappy baby, wailing lusty cries.

Tiny Joseph was so still. His chest moved up and down in labored breathing even though he had an oxygen canula in his nose. The baby boy reminded Adam of the Englisher dolls in the stores at Christmas only with a round face similar to his. After a few minutes, the doctor said he wanted to take Adam to see Emma.

When they entered Emma's room, Adam rushed to her bed and took her hand.

She gave him a weak smile.

"We just came from checking on your babies. How are you feeling?" Dr. Christensen asked.

"Weak and tired recht now, but that will change when I mend and get my energy back," Emma declared. "How are the babies doing?"

Emma teared up when the doctor explained the baby boy was tiny and frail compared to his sister. His heartbeats were weak and his breathing labored. They would have to wait and see if he improved. He had a real fight ahead of him.

Adam shared on his notepad that he just saw the babies in their incubators. Mary was crying, and Joseph was sleeping.

"Is the baby girl hungry, Doctor?" Emma asked looking worried.

"It hasn't been that long since you fed her so I wouldn't think so. The boy didn't nurse I understand," the doctor said. "The nurses in care of the babies today mentioned that the baby girl has good lungs. They weren't sure what to do to make her stop crying."

"Doctor, I think I know," Emma said. "You have the babies separated?"

"Yes, that's right," he said.

"The sonograms showed Mary has been holding Joseph's hand, trying to comfort him because he does not feel gute. They have never been separated before. Mary cannot see how the baby boy is doing. I do not like to see them parted when Joseph needs his sister, and Mary needs to be with him. Could you put them in the same incubator and let her hold his hand if she wants to?"

The doctor gave her a kindly smile. "I will arrange it, and let you know if that makes Mary quiet down. She needs her rest, and you need yours. Nurses will be taking you to the babies soon to let them nurse."

On Emma's first visit to the Neonatal unit, Mary sucked greedily until she had her fill. She was dozing off as the nurse placed her back in the incubator.

Tiny Joseph's eyes were open when the nurse gave him to Emma. She touched his cheek with a finger. "Hello, Joseph. My, how you look like your daed. You have his eyes and round face." She placed the nipple in his mouth. The baby held on a second and let go."

"He is not trying to nurse," Emma said desperately.

The nurse suggested, "See if you can squeeze milk out the end of the nipple so he gets a taste of it. That might help him get the idea what he's supposed to do."

Emma did as instructed and tried Joseph again. This time, he sucked, although weakly. Emma sighed deeply. She was so relieved to see him try. She smiled at the nurse and got a thumb up in return.

Several times through the night, a nurse woke Emma to let the babies nurse. Each time, Mary sucked longer than Joseph. However, Emma was encouraged when Joseph's sucking action grew stronger, and he drank longer.

The next morning Emma was in such a hurry to see the babies, the nurse had a hard time keeping her in bed until the wheelchair arrived. As soon as an orderly brought the chair in, the nurse transferred Emma and pushed her to the Neonatal unit.

The nurse went after the babies while Emma waited in the small room off the unit. She pushed the incubator out the door and stopped by Emma.

Mary was sleeping peacefully. She had a good hold on her brother's hand. The nurse said, "You were right about her wanting to be near her brother. She's sleeping well now in the same incubator with him."

"She is still holding Joseph's hand I see," Emma said, smiling.

"Yes, but if she doesn't find his hand on her own, she gets unhappy so we put their hands together," the nurse said.

"Denki, for doing that," Emma replied.

The nurse handed her Joseph first. His chest was thumpy, and his complexion ashen.

"Joseph does not look as gute today as he did yesterday," Emma fretted.

The nurse shook her head. "We tried to give him some water, but he let what we gave him run back out. We're afraid we might choke him."

"Let me see if he will nurse," Emma said.

"He's so tiny and weak right now. Don't get your hopes up. He might not have the strength to suck," the nurse warned.

Emma's eyes moistened. "He sucked during the night."

"I saw that in report. See what happens," the nurse said. She tightened the blanket around Joseph, unlatched his sister's hand and lifted him carefully from the incubator.

Emma held out her arms for him. She sheltered the baby against her and talked softly to him. He opened his eyes and stared at her as if he understood what his mother said. Emma pulled her gown open and stuck the nipple in the baby's mouth. She rubbed his cheek softly as she willed him to nurse. Just when she was about to give up, the baby's cheeks made in and out sucking movements. The nurse and Emma could hear the faint sounds as he swallowed.

The nurse gasped. "Look at him go. He must not like the water we tried to feed him."

Emma suggested, "Maybe it was the artificial nipple on the bottle he did not like."

Just as quickly as Joseph started nursing, he stopped when he heard his sister give a wailing cry. He listened and puckered up, making weak squeaking sounds to answer her.

Emma laughed. "Mary woke up and found her brother missing. See Joseph's face. He will not nurse now. Put Mary on my lap. I will let her nurse at the same time. Maybe Joseph will try again."

Emma was pushed back to her room when the babies fell asleep. In two hours, the nurse brought Emma back to let the babies nurse again. That time, Emma felt encouraged when she noticed that Joseph's face was rosy.

For the next two days, Emma held her babies and let them nurse at the same time. Joseph seemed to perk up and respond quicker with each nursing, but he always needed the oxygen to help him breathe.

When Doctor Burns made his rounds, he checked on Emma. He said she could be released the next morning. Baby Mary was in good enough condition to go home with her. Baby Joseph would have to stay in the hospital where he had special care.

"I cannot separate my two babies. Mary being with Joseph is what keeps him going. I am sure of it. Mary is not happy the minute they are parted. The twins have to stay together. Do you still think that Joseph is not going to live?" She asked bluntly.

"His chances are not good. Yes, I don't expect him to live long," the doctor said.

"I see. I want to talk to Nurse Hal before I leave the hospital and see what she thinks I should do," Emma said.

When Adam came, Emma asked him to bring Hal to her. She wanted her step-mother's medical opinion about what to do for the twins. After discussing the situation with Hal, Emma and Adam made their decision. When Doctor Burns made his rounds, Emma told him as soon as he released the baby girl from the hospital the baby boy was coming home with them.

Doctor Burns slowly shook his head. "Not a good idea. You should leave the boy here. He needs to be on oxygen and watched all the time. You must heal and get your strength back. You can't do that and take care of the twins when one is a special needs baby."

"I do not think Joseph will nurse for the nurses. I cannot be home with Mary and here with him. They are not happy apart which makes me worry that Mary will not thrive without Joseph. Can you send oxygen home with us?"

"Yes, but you can't stay awake day and night to care for these babies and watch the baby boy for changes in his condition," Doctor Burns said.

"I will have plenty of gute help in Nurse Hal and my mammi. They will help me take care of the babies around the clock. We want to have Joseph with us as long as possible. He needs to feel his family's love as well as his sister's," Emma explained. "If he is going to be with God soon, we want him to leave from his home in the arms of his loved ones and not this hospital."

Doctor Burns scratched a sideburn as he thought. "It's your decision. In most cases, I'd say no, but this time I think you might be right."

The next morning, Adam pulled the buggy in front of the emergency doors. He climbed out and opened the back of the buggy so he could pull the empty cradle close.

Hal checked her sleeping baby in his cradle before she went in to help Emma get ready to leave. She wheeled the new mother outside and helped her onto the seat in back so she could watch the babies. Two nurses came out carrying the twins, placed them gently in the cradle and set Joseph's oxygen tank beside the cradle.

On the way home, Adam drove slower than usual so as not to make the ride rough. He turned in at their house just as the twins set up a wail.

Hal laughed. "I think we got home just in time. These two sound hungry to me. Hurry up and get them inside. You need to feed them, Emma, before they wake Johnnie up."

Jim and Nora sat on the front porch, waiting for them. Emma gave each of them a hug and thanked them for helping.

Nora laughed. "I fixed lunch. Your grandfather's contribution was to pace the floor, waiting to see the new great grandbabies."

"He will not only get to see them, he might have to have cotton plugs in his ears as loud as they are crying," Emma joked.

"Ah, but that's music to my ears," Jim said as he peered in the blankets, first at Mary in Adam's arms and at Joseph in Emma's arms.

"Dad, I have a job for you. How about you go get the two cradles in the back of the buggy so these little ones and Johnnie can have their bed back," Hal said.

After lunch, the daily routine was worked out by Hal and Nora. While Tootie cooked for Jim and Hal's family, Hal and Nora would watch the babies around the clock so Emma could rest.

Mary waited two hours between eating, but Joseph had to eat about every hour. When he cried, he woke up Mary. The minute he left her side, she showed her concern for him with sympathy whimpering. To keep her from fretting, Mary had to be laid on Emma's lap even when she didn't want to eat.

Chapter 15

On one of Hal's mornings away from Emma's house, she stopped at the Tefertiller farm to see how Priscilla was feeling. When Hal caught Priscilla up about the twins, she was determined to visit Emma that very day.

"Emma will be glad to have your company. While you visit with her, I've got tons of work that needs to be done at my house. You tell Emma I'll be back in time to make lunch," Hal said.

"I will tell her. I see you have shed your cast," Priscilla told her.

"Jah and I am very glad to be rid of it," Hal declared. "I have too much to do to drag that heavy cast around."

As Hal predicted, Emma was delighted to see Priscilla. "Ach, I am so glad you came to visit me. Adam and I have been so tied down lately, taking care of two babies. Denki to Hallie and Mammi for helping me. Sometimes, taking care of the babies is overwhelming for this new mama."

"I think I am about to find out how that feels. It is about time I thought about someone besides myself. You have been so gute to me. Hal stopped this morning to update me about the twins. I told her I was coming recht over to see them. She said tell you she would be back this afternoon. Can I see them?" Priscilla asked.

Emma rose slowly from her rocker. "Sure enough, come with me." She led the way to the dining room table near the heating stove. "Sorry it is so warm in here, but we keep a light fire in the stove to keep the babies from losing body heat." She pointed at the larger twin. "Mary is doing fine, but sure enough, Joseph finds life a daily struggle. We could not separate them so we brought them home even though the doctor advised Joseph stay put. Sure enough, the doctor thought the baby should die in the hospital. Adam and I disagreed. See how peaceful he is with Mary beside him, and Mary as long as she knows he is with her."

"I see. How tiny he is. Is his health improving any at all?" Priscilla asked.

"Not very much. It is a day by day battle for the poor little one. As bad as I wanted to bring my baby girl home, her brother needs her worse recht now so we brought them home to feel their families love for them. If Joseph leaves us and goes to Heaven, Mary is going to be hard to console for a while I am afraid," Emma said. "Ach! Enough about us.

You look like you are feeling so much better. Would you please try coming back to work? I was filling in once in a while, but the babies need my attention now. Mary is eating ever three hours, but Joseph eats every hour or two around the clock. Adam will have to find another clerk if you do not come."

"I do not know if I can work in the shop after what happened. Besides, by late fall I will have my baby and need some time off," Priscilla said, laying her hand on her expanding stomach.

"I already have that time figured out," Emma said. "Sure enough, I will be doing well so I will fill in for you while you are on bed rest. When you are able to come to work again after the baby can travel you bring it to work with you. When the baby needs to eat, you can disappear upstairs until the baby is done nursing. Same with a diaper change.

I had thought I could take these babies to the shop and do the same, but they are so frail yet. I cannot see very far ahead, because they grow slowly. No telling how long Joseph will need oxygen and special care. Maybe always," Emma's eyes misted up. "Maybe he is going to leave soon for Heaven like the doctors said. We just do not know."

Priscilla put an arm around Emma's shoulders and gave her a piercing gaze. "You have been giving this much thought. All recht, if you think the customers will not mind who is behind the counter, I will give it a try. Have you considered I just might be bad for Adam's business if customers think of me as second hand goods."

"That is nonsense. No one that knows you thinks that way. The English customers do not know you so they have no thought at all. They only come to the shop to buy Adam's furniture," Emma protested.

Priscilla's face took on a haunted look as she touched Mary's cheek with a finger. "I just wish that awful man's trial was over, and he was in prison now. I do not know if I have the nerve to face him in court to testify against him."

"I have the nerve. We can see if only my testimony will be enough and maybe yours in writing. That is if the trial is delayed until I do not have to worry so much about my babies," Emma said. "Have you heard from Bobby lately?"

"Nah! I have not seen him since I told him I was pregnant. I did not think he would want to marry me once he knew about the baby. Bobby said he had to decide what was best for the two of us, and he would let me know. I have not heard from him since. Ach, I guess it is just as well. I understand this is my problem and not his," Priscilla said sadly.

Hal walked in on the conversation. "Priscilla Tefertiller, you are much too hard on yourself. Don't be so sure about Bobby. Give him a chance to think over your future together. I'll bet Bobby is missing you recht now. I am sure of it.

Now let's get Emma back off her feet. She needs all the rest she can get before one or the other of the twins wake up."

As soon as Emma was settled in the rocker, it was as if the babies sensed it was feeding time. The cradle filled with sounds of grunts and squeaks.

"I spoke too soon. Emma, get ready for company." Hal started back to the cradle. Priscilla followed. "Can I take baby Mary to Emma? I would be nervous holding Joseph as fragile as he is."

"Sure you can," Hal said as she picked up Joseph and his oxygen canister.

Emma held her arms open for the babies to be settled on her lap. Soon she was nursing two contented babies with Joseph's oxygen canister penned between her hip and the rocker.

Hal sat in Adam's rocker close to Emma. "Now if you would sit down on the couch, Priscilla, I've a story I'd like to tell you and Emma." A wail came from the cradle on the other end of the table. "Ach, wait a minute until I get Johnnie. He has decided if the other two babies are eating it is his meal time, too."

"Hal, don't get up. You look like you need to rest. I can bring you Johnnie," Priscilla said, heading for the table.

"I think that's a splendid offer. I'll just let you," Hal said.

"Sure enough," Priscilla said, "I can stay for a while and do some work around here while you both rest if that is all recht?"

"I'd love to have your company. You do not have to work," Emma said.

"I do not mind helping. Just tell me what you need done," Priscilla offered.

"I'll be glad to tell you what we need done," Hal chimed in, "But first sit down, Priscilla, and listen to my story. It's about my own parents and how give and take made their marriage a loving success. All couples should try so hard. There would be less divorces.

My parents owned a farm near Titonka in northern Iowa until they moved here. When I was seven, my mom worked at a women's dress shop in town to make extra money to help out on the dairy farm.

One morning, she burnt the toast. I guess the toaster was going haywire so it wasn't her fault. That morning, Mom was in a hurry to get to work so she served Dad and me the burnt toast. Dad ate the black toast with his bacon and eggs and didn't say a word. I took my cue from him, covered mine with strawberry jam and choked it down.

Mom was always in a hurry first thing in the morning.

She'd be urging me to get ready for school and fixing breakfast so she could leave for work as soon as the school bus picked me up.

In the evening, Mom would be about out on her feet as she made supper for us after a very long and rough day at work. During the Christmas season, the stores stayed open longer. That meant Mom's hours were longer.

At supper, she placed a plate with scrambled eggs and extremely burned toast in front of my dad and me. Not slightly burnt but toast completely blackened. I'd suffered through the piece that morning and didn't want to eat another one. I waited to see if Dad would tell Mom she needed to watch the toaster closer or buy a new one.

To my surprise, Dad slattered a lot of strawberry jam on his toast and ate like he liked his toast charred. As usual, his conversation ran the same most nights. Had the store been really busy that day for mom? How had my day gone? Did I have my homework done yet?

I don't remember how I answered him that night, I do remember my mom apologized to Dad for burning the toast. It was like when she stared into her plate, fixed just like ours, she woke up. She didn't want to eat the burnt toast either.

I'll never forget what my dad said: "Sweetie, I love burned toast. Don't give it another thought."

Later that night after I finished my homework in my room, I went to the living room to tell my parents good night. Dad was reading the newspaper, and Mom was doing dishes in the kitchen. I whispered when I asked him if he really liked his toast burned.

He put his arm on my shoulder and spoke softly so Mom couldn't hear him, "Your momma put in a very long day at work, and she was very tired. Besides, burnt toast now and then never hurts anyone, but you know what does? Harsh words to someone who loves us and does so much for me and you! He went on to say You know, life is full of imperfect things and imperfect people. I'm not the best at hardly anything, and I forget birthdays and anniversaries just like every other human. It's your mom that helps me out when I need it and remembers everyone's birthday for me. She never once has complained about helping me.

What I've learned over the years is that learning to accept each others faults and choosing to celebrate each other's differences, is one of the most important keys for creating a healthy, growing, and lasting relationship between a man and woman. Life is too short to wake up with regrets. Love all the people who treat you right, Hallie, and have compassion for the ones who don't.' That's what Dad told me." Hal looked down at her contented sleeping baby. "Sure enough, I've put Johnnie to sleep. Enough with story telling. I hope it helps both of you some how."

Priscilla studied her hands clasped in her lap, thinking. Hal hoped the young woman was thinking about Bobby right now and how she felt about him.

Emma had an eyebrow arched and a wondering look on her face.

Hal smiled at her and winked. Emma nodded that she understood. Hal said, "Priscilla, put Johnnie back in his cradle for me, and come to the kitchen. We have lunch to cook for Adam and us. He comes home mid day to check on his twins and Emma."

Right at noon, Adam opened the back door easy and slipped into the kitchen. He waved his greeting. Right behind him was Bobby.

Bobby froze with a deer in the headlights look when he saw Priscilla coming to the table with a bowl of mashed potatoes. She placed the bowl before she calmly said, "Just in time. Hal has lunch ready."

"I ---I do not have to stay," Bobby stammered, his face turning pink. "I just came to see the twins."

Adam whipped his notepad out. "You came. You stay."

"Nonsense, Bobby, Priscilla and I made plenty to eat." Hal declared as she took him by the arm and walked him through the kitchen doorway. She ordered, "You stay and eat with us. Wash up and sit down while the food is hot, men. The babies are sleeping. You can see them after you eat."

"I will see what is keeping Emma." Priscilla rushed past

the men and went to help Emma place the babies in their cradle. "Adam brought Bobby home with him. Maybe I should go home," she whispered.

"Sure enough, why would you do that?" Emma asked.

"I do not want to make Bobby uncomfortable in your house. He said he came to see the babies. He did not expect me to be here," Priscilla whispered.

"You have as much recht here as he does. You are my friend and my company, ain't so?"

"Jah, but ---." Priscilla started to protest.

Emma took Priscilla's arm much like Hal did Bobby and pulled her to the kitchen. "I do not want to hear buts. I am hungry."

Adam wobbled his hand at Emma and pointed to the other room.

Emma said, "About the same. Mary is doing great, but not much change in Joseph. He eats like a bird so far. They are sleeping recht now as well as Johnnie."

Adam's face took on a sad look.

Priscilla felt so bad for Adam and Emma. She wanted to help them. "Adam, Emma and I have been talking. Would you like me to come back to work at the shop?"

Adam studied her and nodded.

"I could start in the morning if you want," Priscilla said.

Again Adam nodded.

"I do not promise how I will feel when I get inside. I have not stepped foot in the shop since --- since --- you know," she faltered, looking at her plate.

Adam snapped his fingers to get her attention. Priscilla looked and watched him wobbled his hand as he gave her a gentle smile.

"All recht, I will try in the morning," Priscilla said with little conviction now that she gave thought to what happened to her in the shop.

Bobby was quiet all through lunch. He darted a look at Priscilla several times and caught her watching him. They both quickly looked down at their plates.

After lunch, the men went into the living room to see the

babies and left out the front door. Priscilla helped Hal clean up the kitchen. When they were finished, she said she should leave. She needed to go home and get prepared for her first work day in the morning.

Hal sat down on the couch and leaned back to rest before Johnnie woke up. Emma sat in her rocker with her legs stretched out.

Hal smiled. "Listen! Isn't that quiet a blessing? We could hear a pin drop recht now."

"Jah, it is soothing on the nerves after the lunch we just endured," Emma said.

"I sure was surprised to see Bobby," Hal said through a yawn.

Emma chuckled. "No more than Priscilla was. I thought she was going to run out of here before I got her calmed down. I am sure tonight I will hear Adam's thoughts on Priscilla being here when he invited Bobby. He would rather that did not happen."

"I'm glad you talked Priscilla into staying. Maybe just being together with us helped break the ice between those two. They do need to be together. If Bobby wasn't so schtaerkeppich (stubborn) maybe he'd win her back," Hal said adamantly.

"I agree, but what is that old saying about we can only lead horses to water," Emma said sagely.

"I know. We can't make them drink. I hear ya," Hal agreed, feeling her eye lids getting heavy.

Emma watched Hal doze off. *Gute, she needs to rest.* Easing out of the rocker, she went to the cradle to check on the twins. They were warm enough. Mary, with her belly full, slept soundly. She had her hand on Joseph's arm. Joseph was asleep, but as always, he breathed hard like he struggled to get each breath.

Emma smiled as she picked Mary's tiny wrist up and put her hand down beside her. She wanted to hold Joseph just to be near him in the few minutes she had to herself. Mary wasn't good at sharing her brother. She cried pitifully any time they were separated. Maybe she could sneak a turn with him while Mary slept.

Emma carried the baby and his oxygen tank back to her rocker. As she slowly rocked, she heard the soft swishes the rocker made against the floor. This was how it was meant to be for her and her babies.

Tears misted in her eyes as she held the tiny baby close. She wished she'd be able to watch him grow up with Mary. She didn't think prayer was going to make a difference now. Was it too much to keep asking God for a miracle? He had let her baby live long enough to come home. Why couldn't God let Joseph stay where he was loved by so many people?

She didn't want to think about the stress that would be put on Mary if Joseph was to die? Baby Mary wouldn't be the only one to miss Joseph. His daed and mama didn't want to be without him either. Yet, as she gently laid her hand on his tiny chest, she felt the struggle he had trying to take each breath and the fast beats of his heart, thumping so hard to keep him alive.

God, please help me be strong no matter what you decide. I know whatever happens is Your will, but I am not going to like giving You back this baby. I thought I could suffer through the loss before I held him in my arms. Now that I have had time to love this tiny precious soul it will be hard for me to give him up to You. God, please let me keep him, take care of him, love him and watch him grow up.

Chapter 16

The next morning, Priscilla harnessed her horse to the fiberglass buggy and drove to the Keim furniture shop. Dread consumed her the minute she got to the shop door. She sucked in an unsteady sigh when she opened the door and heard the bell jingle. Inside, she stared at the counter. Panic simmered in her eyes. Hugging herself, she walked back and forth by the front windows, reliving in her mind all that happened to her behind that counter.

Adam saw her pacing from his workshop behind the shop. He came to Priscilla and stood in front of her with an eyebrow raised.

Priscilla's face was pasty white with fear. "Adam, I thought I could do this, but I am not sure now. I am so sorry, but I have to get out of here for a little bit. I am going for a walk in the timber to get some fresh air and think about this. Maybe I should go to my rock and pray for more courage than I feel recht now."

"That is all recht," Adam wrote on his pad. "This has not been a busy day. You want me to go with you?"

Priscilla already had her hand on the door knob. "Denki, Adam. I just need to be alone. I will not stay long."

Adam waved bye.

Priscilla hurried out the door and walked across the grassy patch. The timber looked as peaceful and as inviting as ever. She'd always felt safe among the trees. She picked her way through the brush on a path she was sure only she and the deer used. When she reached the clearing, she knelt by the split rock.

With one hand on the rock to study her, she raised her tear stained face and looked up at the patches of clear blue sky showing between the branches on the oak trees. "How can I go on with my life from here, Lord, if I cannot even be comfortable enough to work in the furniture shop? I am no gute to Adam and Emma as much as I want to help them if I cannot stand being in Adam's shop.

If I am to look forward to the future, show me how to plan according to your will and not just my own. I need your help."

Plunking noises around her sounded loud in the quiet as acorns hit dried grass. *If so much noise is any sign, there must be a gute crop of acorns for the squirrels and wild turkeys this winter.*

The undeniable rustling sound of a deer or human walking through the dried leaves grew louder, coming toward her. Priscilla plastered herself against the rock, waiting to see what or who would appear.

"Do not be scared of me. I would never hurt you. I came by the shop to see how your morning was going, and to tell you it was gute to see you yesterday. Adam said maybe I would find you here." Bobby sat down on the ground by her.

Priscilla let the silence settle, not wanting to make small talk. She couldn't think of a thing to say that would be different from their other talks.

Bobby finally broke the silence. "Working at the shop proved to be harder than you thought I guess."

"Jah," Priscilla said shortly.

Bobby frowned at her. "Sure enough, I am worried about you. At least, you could talk to me."

Priscilla looked away as she shrugged. "I would rather be alone."

Bobby grabbed her by the shoulders and turned her to face him. "Listen to me. You have to quit shutting me out of your life. I care about you. We cannot undo what happened to you. No matter how much I would like to help you forget the past that is impossible. We both have to go on and face the future. Not dwell on the past."

Priscilla tried not to flinch under his penetrating gaze. "I am having trouble doing that. We were so happy. Me and you. God let that man harm me and ruined everything for us. Now I carry that evil person's baby. I feel like I am not allowed to forget and move past what happened. I face that awful day every time the baby kicks. Later on, I will still face what happened to me when I look at this baby I did not want."

Bobby pleaded, "You do not have to live with this alone if you let me help you. The two of us can put what happened so far back in our thoughts that you will be happy with me again. I just know you can."

"How can you be so sure?" She questioned.

"Do you want to keep the baby or give it up?" Bobby asked.

"Would it matter to you which way I choose?" Priscilla countered.

"If you marry me, I will support you no matter what you decide. We can see the baby gets a gute home if you cannot take care of it, or I will help you raise the baby. It is your decision to make," Bobby said.

"You make it sound like such a simple decision. I feel as if I should keep the baby. It is half me, but I cannot be sure if that is what I will do once the baby is born.

You would blame God for something dreadful in your life, ain't so? In fact ,I did not know you several years ago very well, but when Annie died I heard you were bitter just like I am now," Priscilla accused.

"Jah, I was upset for a time sure enough. Finally, I moved on, but my life was empty until I kept company with you," Bobby said truthfully, taking his hands away from her shoulders. "We have been taught to believe what happens in our lives is God's will. The bishop read me a passage from chapter fifty-five in Isiah. He told me to tell you about it. Do you want to hear it?"

Jah, tell me if you must," Priscilla said, giving a labored sigh.

"It goes, '*For my thoughts are not your thoughts, neither are your ways my ways, saith the Lord. For as the heavens are higher than the earth, so are my ways higher than your ways, and my thoughts than your thoughts.*' Priscilla, you can understand that, ain't so?"

"Jah, the Lord did not tell that man to attack me or condone his evil act, but I feel so confused. I need help renewing my faith. I need the recht spirit in me again, before I am fit company for you," Priscilla said.

"I can help you if you let me. Lean on my strength to help the Lord renew your strength and faith. We will do it together as a couple," Bobby insisted.

Priscilla nodded. "All recht, but I will not promise anything recht now. I need to take the days slowly, one at a time."

"We have to start somewhere, but I better warn you, I will get ladich (tired) of courting you after a time. I will wish for you to hurry up and marry me and have it done with once and for all," Bobby declared. "Now you want to go back to the shop? I will go with you if you are uneasy and stay until closing time so Adam can work on his order of furniture."

"You would do that for me? Emma offered to stay with me when we first talked about me coming back to work, but she is not up to it now. You surely have your own work to do," Priscilla rebuked.

Bobby bobbed his head sideways. "I am not that busy until harvest starts. Gute, that is settled. I want to stay with you. In no time, working at the shop will come easy once you make it through a day or two, ain't so?"

"Jah, as far as work goes I guess so, but think ahead. If you are going to spend time with me, you will watch me grow larger with another man's child. Now it is my turn to ask you something. Have you really come to a decision about this baby I carry?" She asked pointedly.

Bobby nodded. "Jah, I want you to marry me soon, before you become any larger. I was telling you the truth when I said if you decide to keep the baby I will abide by that. No more needs to be said about this. We will raise the baby together."

"Are you so sure you can do that with everyone knowing about how I came by this baby?" Priscilla pushed.

Bobby rubbed the rock a few seconds, hoping it would be his inspiration like it was Priscilla's, as he figured out how to respond. He looked Priscilla in the eyes. "People have short memories. Soon they will have something new to talk about.

You mentioned my feelings for Annie. Remember Annie had a baby. I knew how that baby was conceived, and I still asked Annie to marry me. I intended to raise Beth as my own, but that did not work out. When Annie was killed, Nurse Hal was already raising Beth with Redbird so it was best she kept the girl. This baby you are carrying is half you, and it will get all your goodness and both our love.

Bishop Bontrager pointed out to me that Joseph knew Mary was having a child that was not his and he loved her enough to stay with her. Could I do no less now when I want to be with the woman I love?"

Priscilla's eyes filled with tears as she looked up again through spaces in the trees at the bright blue spots. "Bobby, do you ever stop to look at the blueness of the sky or take in the smells on the breeze that just kicked up? Notice the way the tiny white clouds build on the horizon and turn into cotton mountains, drifting slowly like they are in no hurry? How about the sea of yellow in the grass when dandelions bloom? So much recht around this rock to enjoy."

Bobby looked overhead. "Nah, I had not paid any attention to the sky or flowers, but those things wonder me when I see them through your eyes. How is it that you notice these things?" Bobby asked.

Priscilla swiped the tears off her cheeks with the back of her hands. "There was a long time I didn't pay attention to my surroundings. Try staying shut up in a dark room for days. It will make you wonder about all that you missed. When I escaped from my self imposed prison, the first thing I did was sit in the porch rocker. I saw so clearly the sights around me that I had missed for months."

Bobby took her hand. He was encouraged when she did not pull away. He helped her to her feet. "Priscilla, do not change the subject. You were the woman I wanted to spend my life with before this awful thing happened to you. You still are the one I want in my home as my wife, spending the rest of my life with me. I love and respect you for your strength to keep your baby. I want to marry you," Bobby vowed.

"It gives me hope to hear you say it is so," Priscilla said, giving him a kiss on the cheek.

"Ach, I just proposed. What is your answer?" Bobby asked.

Priscilla crossed her arms over her chest. "Nah, you said you wanted to marry me. There was no question for me to answer. You did not ask me to marry you."

Bobby ran his fingers through his hair. "You are really trying to be difficult. All recht, Priscilla Tefertiller, will you marry me?"

"Jah, I will marry you because I love you. We can raise the baby together, because together we are stronger. We can do anything if it is together. We will leave this to God's will and see what happens," Priscilla said as if she was reciting. "Is that what you want to hear?"

"Not just what I want to hear. You have to feel that it is recht," Bobby said. His forehead filled with worry creases.

"Jah, I feel marrying you is recht after you have been so patient with me," Priscilla said.

Bobby picked her up and whirled her around. "Let's go tell, Adam, Emma and Mama."

He placed her feet back on the ground and took her hand to hurry her through the timber. "We can tell them later, Bobby. Recht now take me back to the shop before Adam fires me for skipping out."

Priscilla's mind raced as fast as her feet. *Bobby, you are asking for miracles from me I do not feel will happen. If you would just listen to what I try to tell you and not insist on what you want to hear me say. With as mixed up as I am, I may not make a gute wife. I am not and may never be the same woman you fell in love with. Something tells me I might not be able to love the baby I am carrying. I pray the baby is a girl. That might help if she looks like me. I will marry you soon and see what happens as time goes by. In the future if moments of fear and darkness keep enveloping me to torment me, you may be very sorry you took me as your wife.*

About The Author

Fay Risner lives with her husband on a central Iowa acreage with their chickens, rabbits, goats and cats. A former Certified Nurse Aide at the Keystone Nursing Care Center in Keystone, Iowa, she now divides her time between writing books, working in her flower beds and the garden and going fishing with her husband in their boat. Fay writes books in various genre and languages – historical mystery series, western series, Amish series set in southern Iowa and two books for Caregivers about Alzheimer's. She uses 12 font print in her books and 14 font print in her novellas to make them reader friendly. Her books have a mid western Iowa and small town flavor. She pulls the readers into her stories, making it hard for them to put a book down until the reader sees how the story ends. Readers say the characters are fun to get to know and often humorous enough to cause the readers to laugh out loud. The books leave the readers wanting a sequel or a series so they can read about the characters again.

Enjoy Fay Risner's books and please leave a review to make other readers familiar with her work.

Book Discussion Group Questions

1. What did you enjoy about this book?
2. What have you read that is similar to this book?
3. What are some of the major themes of this book?
4. What do you think the author was trying to accomplish with this novel?
5. Who was your favorite character? What did you appreciate about him/her?
6. Consider the main character: what does he/she believe? What is he/she willing to fight for?
7. At the end of the book, do you feel hope for the characters?
8. What is stronger in the book: plot or character development? Why? Do you think this was intentional on the part of the author?
9. Have you ever experienced anything similar to the action of this novel?
10. Did you find this book a quick read? Why or why not?
11. What are your concerns about this book?
12. How did you feel about the main character?
13. What are the most important relationships in the book?
14. What makes a minor character memorable?
15. What are the most revealing scenes?
16. Are any of the events in the book relevant to your own life?
17. What did you think of the style of the writer?
18. Was the story credible? The characters credible?
19. Did you find any flaws in the book?